HEIDI'S FRIENDS

Heidi gathered wild flowers, as many
as her arms could hold

HEIDI'S FRIENDS

A Sequel to "Heidi"

ADAPTED FROM ORIGINAL STORIES

By JOHANNA SPYRI

Illustrations by

SERGIO LEONE

GROSSET & DUNLAP *Publishers*

NEW YORK

LIBRARY OF CONGRESS CATALOG CARD NO. 65-18972
PRINTED IN THE UNITED STATES OF AMERICA

Contents

Contents

Illustrations

HEIDI'S FRIENDS

CHAPTER I

Before the Journey

A BLUSTERING south wind shook the tops of the ancient fir trees and stirred among the bluebells that lined the steep mountain path. Golden sunbeams flashed here and there on the twin peaks above, then quickly became obscured by gray shadows, for the mighty wind was driving great flying clouds every moment across the sun.

Forced first away from the wind, then towards it, a little girl with bright red cheeks and flying black curls, her eyes full of the joy of life, was racing down the mountain. The round hat belonging on her head was hanging from her arm, and was swinging back and forth so violently in the swift descent that at any moment it was in danger of being torn from its ribbon.

Now the whistling wind retreated somewhat, and under the trees it became more quiet. The little girl stopped running and looked up at the branches above her. There, where the wind had more room, it blew with great force, and its shaking and roaring up in the top must have awakened in the child a strange impulse to give expression to her energy. Suddenly she rushed towards the contrary blowing wind and struggled and resisted and ran against its force. Then she abruptly turned around. Driven by the wind, she dashed down the steep edge of the meadow to where, somewhat sheltered from the wind, a little wooden house overlooked the green slope.

The little girl must have been well known here. In three high jumps, she reached the door.

"Grandmother! Grandmother!" she called into the house. "Have you noticed how jolly the wind is to-day?"

An old woman with gray hair and a cap securely tied over it came towards her, tapping her cane as she came.

"You are right, Heidi," she exclaimed, clasping the child's hands in welcome, "the wind is jolly, so long as the Alm Uncle's strong nails hold and it does not tear the roof from over our heads. Just the same, I prefer to remain inside. I have a bit of spinning to do before Brigitte comes in from the shed to make Peter's supper. He will be hungry after spending all day in the pasture with the goats. I only hope the wind does not blow him away."

"He will lie flat on the ground, Grandmother. He always does that when the wind is blowing," Heidi assured her. "It blows so hard that you have to lie on the ground or struggle with all your might if you don't want to fly away like the birds and then be blown down the whole mountain. You ought to know how jolly it is outside."

"I would rather not know," said the grandmother, withdrawing a little from the blast that came through the open house door and feeling her way as she turned back towards her own sitting room. Her blind eyes could not see the brightly shining pans Brigitte had hung along the wall beside the fireplace or the freshly scrubbed table in the narrow kitchen through which they passed. Beyond, in the sitting room, the grandmother seated herself beside her spinning wheel while Heidi pulled up a little stool.

"I will read you one hymn, Grandmother," she said, taking a worn book down from the shelf by the window, "and then I must hurry on to the village and mail the letter I have in my pocket. There is something in it that concerns you, but this time you may be sure I will not stay away from the Alm. I am only going for a short visit."

"Going? Where to, Heidi?" asked the grandmother, greatly disturbed and reaching for the child's hand to reassure herself. "You will come back?"

"Oh, yes," Heidi answered, "and I shall bring you a splendid present. What would you like to have, Grandmother? What do you want me to bring you?"

"Only yourself, dearest Heidi. Only yourself," the old woman murmured.

"But Grandmother, bringing myself is nothing," protested Heidi. "Wouldn't you like a nice warm shawl? I want to bring something for Mother Brigitte, too. Maybe some bright cloth with flowers on it so that she could cover the chairs and make curtains for the windows. Herr Sesemann says ever so many beautiful things are to be had at the fair in Berne. But what shall I bring for Peter?"

The blind woman shook her head sadly.

"So it is Herr Sesemann and Klara who are taking you away from me!"

"No, no, Grandmother. You have misunderstood. I am going to them," replied Heidi. "The doctor is taking me—but only for a month—because Klara misses me and cries so much that she is losing the strength the dear Lord gave her while we were together here on the Alm. The traveling was too much for her. She does not walk as well as she used to and the good grandmamma, who will be with us, says that if I can come for only a month it will be enough. What do you think, Grandmother? They have rented a house on the Gemmi for the month of August. It is not like going to Frankfurt where there is nothing but walls and windows. On the Gemmi the mountains are quite as beautiful as they are here. And Grandmother, only think! They are even higher. I shall

not be homesick with Klara on the Gemmi." Giving a
little jump of delight, she added, "I can hardly wait!"
"Then God keep you, Heidi. I would not deny you
this pleasure," sighed the grandmother. "But read me one
hymn to comfort me while you are away."

Heidi leafed through the pages of the old hymnbook.
The blind grandmother had once told her that when
Heidi read aloud to her the picture came very clearly
before her blind eyes and it was exactly as if she could
see. So now Heidi was searching for a hymn that would
show her a pleasant picture.

"Here is one about the garden of Zion!" she exclaimed
at last. "Listen:

"Thy Zion is embowered in palms,
And dark green branches bend,
But I will cheer my soul with psalms,
And to their words attend.

"Oh, Grandmother!" cried Heidi in the midst of her
reading. "I wish we could sing it."

"I could not sing with my old voice, dear child," said
the grandmother. "How it would sound! But I remember the tune as you read. It lets me see the palms
with their dark green branches bending."

"The wind outside is bending the dark green branches
of the fir trees and whistling in the pines," said Heidi.
"Can't you hear it? Doesn't it sound like music? I wish I
could sing it. Peter can sing, but he sings only to the
goats."

"Here he is now!" exclaimed the grandmother, whose
keen ears had heard the clattering of the goats' hoofs as
they clambered down over the rocks, tinkling their little
bells.

Giving the grandmother a farewell hug and bidding
good-bye to Peter's mother Brigitte, who had returned to
the kitchen, Heidi ran outside and was immediately surrounded by goats, for they knew her well.

The whole flock was there except Schwänli and Bärli,

"You will come back, Heidi?" the grandmother asked

her grandfather's goats. These two already had been returned to the Alm Uncle, who had lived as a hermit on the mountain until the orphan Heidi came to share his lonely dwelling. It was called the Alm hut by the villagers, who still regarded the Alm Uncle, as they had named him, with something of their old awe. His dense gray eyebrows and long beard did make him look fierce. But to Heidi he was simply Grandfather and the best loved of all the people to whom the happy-hearted little girl had given her affection.

Even the goats responded to her kind heart and loving ways. Nuzzling and pushing one another, they bleated for attention until Peter had to shout to make himself heard.

"So you are here, Heidi! The Alm Uncle is worried. He fears a storm is blowing up and wants you to hurry back up the mountain. I am to take your letter."

Saying this, Peter took it without knowing in the least what it contained, tucked it inside his weather-beaten cap, swung his rod in the air, and started off with the goats which were being returned to their owners in Dörfli.

"Good-bye, Peter," Heidi called a little wistfully after him. "You won't forget my letter?"

"Surely I won't, and good night!" he called back, then trotted along with the goats. In half an hour's time the whole flock stood still by the rear building a few steps from the Inn, which also served as the village post office, for here Peter had to leave the innkeeper's goats.

Kätheli, the innkeeper's brown-haired daughter, ran out to get them. Peter hardly looked at her, for he had no eyes for any girl but Heidi. He merely thrust the letter into her hand. Kätheli looked at it curiously.

"Oh, a letter from Heidi to Herr Kaspar in Wallis! Who is he?"

"Don't know," said Peter and whistled so hard through his fingers that it resounded far down into the valley almost to the walled vineyards of Maienfeld.

From all the scattered houses the children now came running out. Each rushed upon his own goat, and from the houses nearby, one woman and then another seized her little goat by the cord or by the horn, and in a short time the entire flock was separated and each goat in its own stable.

Finally Peter stood alone with the brown one, his own goat Schnecke, which followed him back to the little house on the side of the mountain. Mother Brigitte was waiting for him in the doorway.

"Has all gone well, Peter?" she asked pleasantly, and then led the brown goat to her shed and immediately began to milk her. Peter's mother was a robust woman and cared for everything herself in the house and in the shed and everywhere kept order. When the milking was ended, she went into the little house and said, "Come, Peter, you must be hungry."

She had everything prepared, and the grandmother was already at the table. Peter had only to sit down; Brigitte seated herself next to him, and although nothing stood on the table but the bowl of corn meal mush with the fresh goat's milk poured over it, Peter thoroughly enjoyed his supper. Then he told his mother and grandmother what he had done through the day to protect himself from the wind, and as soon as the meal was ended he went to bed, for in the early dawn he would have to start forth again with the flock.

In this way Peter had already spent five summers. He had been goat boy for so long and had become so accustomed to going to the pastures, sometimes with Heidi but more often alone, that he could think of nothing else. It did not occur to him to ask who Herr Kaspar was or why Heidi was writing to him until the following morning when he found the Alm Uncle sitting on the bench before his hut looking a little lonely.

"Where's Heidi?" Peter asked abruptly. "The wind is not so strong today. Is she coming with me to the pastures?"

The old man started, then shook his head.

"She is gone, Goat General. She is gone to Klara on the Gemmi."

"Then who is Herr Kaspar?" growled Peter. "She wrote a letter to him."

Very quietly the Uncle explained the situation, pausing now and then to take a long puff on his pipe. Herr Kaspar, it seemed, was the guide whose cottage the Sesemanns had rented for the month of August. He could perfectly well give it up at this time because he himself was to be away traveling with strangers, his two boys would be taking care of the big flocks in the mountain pasture, and his wife would live in the attic room and serve the Sesemann family and their guests. In her letter Heidi had said she was leaving with the doctor that morning and would arrive with the Sesemanns, who had previously arranged to meet her in Berne where they had stopped for the fair.

"So now she is gone," concluded Peter and scowled so darkly that the Alm Uncle had to chuckle to himself.

"Don't worry," he said with a sly glance at the tall youth who stood before him, "she will be back in September when school begins."

And so it happened that, for the first time in his life, Peter found himself looking forward with pleasure to the opening day of school. The following morning, when he started off with his flock, he had a book under his arm. For it had entered his head that he might spend his time in the pastures studying his lessons and thus prove to Heidi, when she returned, that he was not the stupid goat boy the villagers believed him to be.

Meanwhile Heidi was nearing the end of her journey through Switzerland. The beautiful flower-studded fields and lofty snow-clad mountains, the green pastures and blue lakes which she had glimpsed through the train windows had made a deep impression on her. Every moment she turned to the good man, sitting beside her, and in expectant tones came the question:

"When are we coming to the Gemmi?"

The gray-haired doctor's kind bright eyes twinkled at the repeated question, but he only replied gently, "Patience, Heidi. Patience."

While they were waiting at Berne, the doctor pointed out some of the sights of the famous old city, particularly the fountains, since he had first met his little water carrier, as he still called Heidi, at a well in Frankfurt.

There was so much to see that Heidi soon grew tired of walking on the hard pavement. Finally she stood still before the high Clock Tower where she gazed in silent wonder at the quaint figures moving around the face of the ancient calendar clock. But when the knight in gold armor struck the big bell to tell them the hour, her impatience returned and her question became more determined and urgent:

"When are we going to meet Klara and go on to the Gemmi?"

At the station Klara was already waiting in silent expectation between her papa and grandmamma. Soon the entire party was seated in the train, Heidi next to Klara, whom she embraced every moment in sheer delight, for now they were on the last lap of their journey. The two friends could hardly wait to climb out of the train and travel on horseback to the high mountains and green fields.

CHAPTER II

On the Gemmi Pass

NOT FAR from the summit of the Gemmi Pass leading from Wallis across to the canton of Berne, a narrow path enters the woods and soon leads to a place where the traveler cannot look without a shudder over the steep wall of rock down into the deep ravine.

On the August evening before Heidi was to arrive, a boy who looked a little like Peter except that he appeared to be much younger, was coming along this wood path. In his hand he held a large red flower which he had to stop every moment to admire.

Coming out into an open place, he continued along a narrow field path leading to the left up a green slope. Here stood two cottages not far apart, each with a small outbuilding behind it, evidently to shelter the animals. One of these sheds was larger than the other, and the cottage with its brand-new door looked more roomy and better kept than its neighbor.

This cottage belonged to the guide Kaspar, who lived in it with his wife and two boys and every year was able to improve something about it. He earned a good deal of money as guide to travelers, and this year his income would be even better with his boys working as shepherds in the high pastures and his wife in service. In his shed stood not only two goats, like all the neighbors, but for the last two years a fine cow also, which furnished him with wonderful milk and butter.

The smaller cottage beyond with its worm-eaten door and shingle roof belonged to the porter, Martin, the big man who, on account of his powerful build, was called "Strong Martin." He lived there with his wife and four little children, and in his small shed behind stood his two goats, whose milk had to feed the entire family.

All through the summer, especially in fine weather, Strong Martin had a good job carrying travelers' luggage over the Gemmi, but he did not earn nearly so much as his neighbor Kaspar, who was often away many days at a time with the mountain climbers.

In front of the new house door, Kaspar's two boys were now standing and were evidently discussing something very important. They were examining, handling, and comparing, with great eagerness, two objects which they held in their hands. The little fellow who had just come out of the woods now stood still and looked full of astonishment at what was going on in front of his neighbors' door.

"Seppli, come look! Look!" one of the two boys called to him.

Seppli drew near, his blue eyes growing wider and wider in amazement at what was being shown to him.

"See what Father brought us from the village," called the larger of the boys again to Seppli, and each of them held up his present before the little fellow's astonished eyes.

What a wonderful sight it was! Chappi and Georgie each held in his hand a large whip, in this country called a *geissel*, or lash. The strong, yet pliable handle was wound round and round with little bands of red leather. The long white lash was of solid braided leather thongs, and on the end hung a firmly twisted cord of yellow silk finished off with a little yellow tassel. This could make a wonderful crack and was called the whiplash. Never in his life had Seppli seen anything so splendid.

"Now, just listen," said Chappi, beginning to swing his whip until it cracked and thundered up and down the valley. Georgie did the same, making it seem to Seppli as if there could be nothing more wonderful in the whole world.

"If only I had a whip with a yellow lash!" said he, taking a deep breath, when the two had finally stopped cracking theirs.

"You will have to wait for it," replied Chappi haughtily, and with one last tremendous crack he ran away with Georgie swinging and cracking his whip behind him.

Seppli stood motionless gazing after the two boys. A heavy weight had fallen on his untroubled heart. He had seen something which he wanted more than he had ever wanted anything in his whole life. Suddenly he began to tear apart the red flower he had found. Then he threw it away, for to have only a red flower and never, never to own a whip with a yellow lash turned Seppli against the flower. It flew far away into the field and he looked after it in silent rage. No one knows how long he would have remained standing there if the door had not opened behind him and a woman stepped out with a big broom in her hand.

"Where are the boys, Seppli?" she asked curtly.

"Gone off with the whips," was the answer, for they were still before his eyes.

"Run and call them home. Be quick!" commanded the woman. "Tomorrow early they will have to go to the mountain and stay there a whole month. The cottage is rented, and there is still much to be done. Run and tell them, Seppli!"

The youngster then ran off with all his might after Chappi and Georgie while the woman continued her sweeping. She was Kaspar's wife and the mother of the two boys, who were giving up their room to Heidi and Klara. Hence the great preparation with the broom, which was not unnecessary, for Chappi and Georgie brought a great deal of dirt into the house.

Very early the following morning a great cracking of whips was to be heard, for at four o'clock Chappi and Georgie were already waiting in front of the cottage for the cows which they were to drive up on the mountain where the big herd was. The two would remain as shepherd boys, and they were so delighted about it that they couldn't make enough noise with their whips.

When their mother had fastened on their knapsacks and admonished them to be good boys, and they had gone away, she went back into the house, and then began to sweep and dust every room and corner, from top to bottom, so there was no end to it the whole day long. The sun had already gone down behind the fir trees when the woman once more wiped off the windows, one after the other, and looked around to see if the cottage was in order. Everything was shining, the windows all around, the table with the slate top, the benches against the walls, and even the floor.

The woman now saw a whole procession of porters, horses, and riders coming up the path from the valley. She ran quickly up the narrow stairs to the attic chamber, put on a clean apron, and placed herself in the doorway in order to receive her guests. The procession stopped, and Herr Sesemann and his good friend, the doctor, helped first Klara's grandmamma and then the children from the horses.

Heidi's feet hardly had touched the ground when she ran to and fro for joy, and did not know which was the most beautiful, the tiny wooden cottage with the little bench in front of the door, the green fields around with the flowers nodding at her, the rushing mountain brook, or the golden evening sunshine on the rocks and fir trees. Klara, too, was filled with admiration and looked around in silent astonishment.

Then they all went inside the cottage, and a new

pleasure began for Heidi, since everything here was so gay and inviting. It was not at all like the big house in Frankfurt where she had silently fought her homesickness fearing that she would seem ungrateful. Here there was no dignified Sebastian, no stern Fräulein Rottenmeier or haughty Tinette. The cottage was not unlike many of the houses in Dörfli.

Seizing Klara by the hand, Heidi ran with her into every corner, calling excitedly, "See! See! There are seats all around the room against the wall, and just see where you can climb up!"

Whereupon Heidi ran quickly up the stairs leading up behind the oven to an opening through which the largest sleeping room was entered. This was a wonderful discovery.

"Klara! Klara!" she called down to her friend, who had not felt equal to the exertion. "I've found the big sleeping room and here is another and another."

She had opened a door into a second chamber with two smaller sleeping rooms in the alcoves on either end. In one of these, two beds stood on either side of an open window. A wooden staircase on the other side went down again into the living room. This made a wonderful circuit which could be made many times a day, and everything about the whole house, inside and out, promised so much that Heidi did not know what she would enjoy the most.

When, at last, she lay in her own bed upstairs in the alcove chamber, and Klara in the bed beside her, and their prayers had been said, Heidi drew a deep sigh and said with the utmost contentment, "Now we are together on the Gemmi!"

The most beautiful summer days now followed, with golden sunshine on the meadows, with cool breezes blowing in the evergreen woods, and with the deep blue sky spread out like a canopy above the rocks and the white, snow-capped mountains.

In a few days Heidi and Klara had discovered all the

lovely spots in the neighborhood where they could lie down and spend the warm afternoon hours agreeably until evening when Klara would be encouraged to take a short stroll with her papa and grandmamma. Usually Heidi skipped on ahead with the doctor. She was more inclined to discover lovely spots than to rest, and while Klara was sitting on the soft moss under the fir trees or on the sunny mountainside, Heidi always had some new place which she wished to explore.

"Oh, Klara, if you could only walk a little farther," she would begin. Then she would proceed to tell her friend a multitude of plans—how they could climb to the fir trees high up on the rocks and see far around, or go deep, deep into the woods, until they came to the big birds that often screamed so frightfully as they soared far above them in the clear blue sky.

Klara would always listen to these daring proposals with interest, but she had been an invalid for so long that she was not ready to undertake anything so strenuous without her papa's permission, and he thought, too, that there were shorter excursions which would be equally pleasant.

"I know where we'll go then," announced Heidi. "Yesterday and again today, a little boy has been standing in front of the cottage over there, and he looks so sad that I really must go over there and make friends with him."

Herr Sesemann agreed to this necessary errand. But Klara had just seen the grandmamma coming out of the house with a basket of knitting materials on her arm and said she would rather stay with her. She had a horror of strange little boys who stared, because they used to stare at her in the same way when she went about in her wheelchair. Heidi understood this so, with the promise that she would be right back, she ran off alone.

Seppli had been standing in the same spot for an hour, gazing at the house opposite. When Heidi reached him she placed herself directly in front of him, put her hands behind her back, and asked in a friendly way, "Are you looking for someone to play with you?"

"No," replied Seppli curtly.

"What do you expect to see that you keep looking over there?" Heidi persisted.

"Nothing," said Seppli.

This answer was not at all satisfactory to Heidi.

"Don't you want to make friends?" she asked. "What is your name?"

"Seppli."

"How old are you?"

"Don't know."

"You must know. Come, stand beside me so—" and Heidi placed herself beside Seppli, and looked at him over her shoulder. He was quite a little shorter, but much chubbier than she was.

"You are not as tall as I am," she said. "You are quite small. I shall soon be ten years old, for I was nine on my last birthday. Perhaps you are six years old."

Seppli took this information without any doubt, for he did not know that he had been seven years old for some time and that he had grown more in breadth than in height.

"Have you any brothers and sisters?" Heidi persisted further. She had seen several younger children playing about the cottage.

"There are four of us," said Seppli.

That was better.

"They are too young to play with you, aren't they?" asked Heidi. "What do you do all day long?"

The boy had to think about this a long time. Finally he said, "I know where there are red flowers."

These words fell like a burning spark into Heidi's heart. Suddenly she saw before her eyes the beautiful pasture on the Alm with its flaming red Alpine roses and crimson century bushes, and everything in her longed for the wonderful flowers.

"Where? Where? Seppli, where are the flowers? Come, let us go there quickly!" And Heidi seized Seppli's hand and pulled him along. But the boy held back.

"There," he said, and pointed with his finger to the woods above.

"Oh, have you been up there in the big forest?" said Heidi expectantly, pulling Seppli along with all her might.

"Yes, and still farther," replied Seppli deliberately without hurrying his steps for he had heavy wooden shoes on his feet.

But Heidi pulled him still harder. She already saw the path through the dark woods, and behind the trees she could imagine the big red flowers glowing and shimmering.

"Come, Seppli, come," she cried as she pulled him along.

They now came past Kaspar's cottage. Inside the doctor had just finished planning the trip he was to make to Frankfurt to close up the lonely house where he had lost first his wife and then his daughter. In Dörfli, not far from the church and the parsonage, stood an old manor house on which carpenters were busily at work. One part of it the doctor was rebuilding and furnishing for himself while Heidi and her grandfather would live in the other part just as they had done the previous winter. The good doctor was feeling very happy about all these plans as Heidi had come to take the place in his heart that his own daughter had filled.

Just as the doctor stepped out on the threshold to look for Heidi, the strange pair came along, Heidi pulling Seppli after her with all her might.

"Here, here! Not so fast!" called the doctor. "Where are you dragging your new friend?"

"Oh, Doctor!" cried Heidi in great eagerness, "he knows where there are such beautiful red flowers just like those on the Alm, and we are going to get them."

*"There," he said, and pointed with his finger to the
woods above*

"No, no," said the good man, taking Heidi by the hand. "That won't do at all. We must all walk together up there in the woods when Klara is stronger. You must make her want to go as much as you do, but not tonight. See, the sun is already low over the fir trees and I must leave for Frankfurt right after supper."

Whereupon he led Heidi into the house while Seppli ran back to his own cottage where he found his father, Strong Martin, splitting big knotty logs into small pieces for the mother to lay on the hearth. The three younger children stood in a row in front of him with big, eager eyes, watching his work.

Seppli, the oldest, now came along, placed himself in the row, and opened his eyes wide. But soon his father pointed to the pieces of split wood on the ground and said in a more gentle voice than one would have expected from such a big, strong man:

"Here, Seppli, take two at a time in your arms and carry them in to Mother so she can cook our potatoes for us."

Seppli immediately did as he was told. But later, when Heidi came out to bid the doctor good-bye and walk with him for a little way along the field path, Seppli was standing just as motionless as before, gazing wistfully in the direction of Kaspar's cottage.

CHAPTER III

The Long Night

THE DAY the doctor was expected to return from Frankfurt, Frau Sesemann came with her big basket filled with sewing cards and knitting to a lovely, shady spot near the house, to spend the hour before the noonday meal with the children.

Klara sat quietly on her mossy seat, and Heidi stood in front of her, telling with great enthusiasm about a bush in the woods, with flaming red flowers, which shone far away through the trees.

"Are you still talking about that bush, Heidi?" Klara exclaimed with some impatience. "Why don't you ask your little friend over there to pick the flowers for you if you want them so much? Then we could sew the cards Grandmamma has brought for us."

"I want to pick them myself," declared Heidi stoutly.

And again she began describing the bush with even more enthusiasm. Her eyes grew bigger and brighter every moment, for the more she talked about it the more plainly she saw it all before her just as it was in the pasture on the Alm, and it seemed as if she were already on the path in the midst of the shimmering flowers.

Finally the grandmamma put aside her knitting and said kindly, "Sit down now, Heidi, and be quiet. I know a story about a flaming red bush and if you will listen, I will tell it to you."

"I'll listen," promised Heidi, but the red flowers Seppli had described were still before her eyes.

The story was about a shepherd, Moses, who led the flock to a mountain.

"And the angel of the Lord appeared to him in a flame of fire," continued the grandmamma. "Moses looked and the angel was standing in the midst of a bush and the bush burned with fire and was not consumed."

"It was a bush of flowers!" said Heidi with conviction.

She was so full of the woods and her flowers that when the story was finished, she could not sit still. The last the grandmamma saw of her she was running towards the house. When a long time had passed and Heidi did not return, Frau Sesemann became uneasy and said:

"Go in quickly, Klara, and call Heidi. There is time for a walk before luncheon."

Klara ran in, but did not come back for so long that Frau Sesemann went in too. It was perfectly still in the house. No one was in the living room, no one in the kitchen! The grandmamma went up the little staircase and softly opened the door of the children's room, thinking Heidi might have gone in there and fallen asleep. No one was there! Through the open door she could see into the large bedroom, but it was quite empty. Herr Sesemann had gone earlier to the village, and the doctor, who shared the room with him, was not expected back until evening.

"Where can she be?" whispered the grandmamma, standing alone in her own upstairs sitting room.

Soon Klara came up from below and told her she had searched for Heidi in the whole house, in every corner, and even in the yard as far back as the woods, but Heidi was not to be found.

Together they climbed to the garret room belonging to Kaspar's wife. The woman was not there, but they

finally found her outside in the vegetable garden where
she was gathering greens for the noonday meal. When
questioned about Heidi, she replied only that she had
seen the child come into the house some time before. But
where could she have gone afterwards?

The whole house was searched once more, then all
around it. Kaspar's wife helped willingly, for she saw
that Frau Sesemann was becoming anxious, but nowhere
was there any trace of Heidi. The noonday meal was
finished quietly without her, and her portion put away.

"We haven't asked next door," Klara suddenly remembered.

So Kaspar's wife ran over to the neighbors' house.
Perhaps they had seen Heidi. But no one was there. The
door was closed and everything still. Then it came to her
mind that Strong Martin was making hay today, high up
above the rocks, and that the whole household had gone
with him. She came back with this information. Frau
Sesemann became more and more uneasy.

"Oh, if I had only gone after her right away!" she
exclaimed regretfully over and over, but this was of no
use. What was to be done? Where should they look for
Heidi?

"She can climb," asserted Klara. "She scrambles over
the rocks as easily as any of Peter's goats when she is at
home with her grandfather."

But the grandmamma, usually so cheerful, was looking
at nothing but the dark side of the picture.

"What will the poor man say if we have lost her?
How will we comfort the blind grandmother on the Alm
or the boy Peter and his mother? Oh, it is not possible
that anything has happened to our Heidi!"

"Couldn't she have followed her new friend, that boy
who keeps looking over here?" suggested Klara.

The more Frau Sesemann thought about this the more
convinced she became that her granddaughter was right.
If only there were someone to send up there immedi-

ately, she lamented, before the doctor returned from Frankfurt and had to be told that Heidi was missing.

Kaspar's wife offered to do this and to come back again as soon as possible, but it was a long and toilsome way; it would take more time than anyone would think from looking up there to the hay field.

Frau Sesemann promised her a handsome reward if only she would go and prevent the doctor from being worried. She told the woman how he had lost first his wife and then his daughter and how Heidi had comforted him and won her way into his heart.

"He is moving to Dörfli on purpose to be near her," continued the grandmamma. "I think, if anything happened to her it would be more than he could bear, after what he's been through. And the dear Lord only knows how her grandfather would take it! Please, good woman, if you can realize our predicament, won't you hurry?"

Kaspar's wife hurried off. She was still very hopeful that she would bring Heidi back with her. But the way was farther than the grandmamma had thought. Long before the obliging woman could return, the doctor bustled in and immediately asked for Heidi. Then everything had to be told him.

At the first great shock the doctor wanted to go out at once to look for the child, but Frau Sesemann was so sure that Heidi must have followed the little boy that he calmed himself and decided to wait for the return of Kaspar's wife. But the poor doctor didn't have a peaceful moment. He paced from one window to the other, then back to the door and around the house. The time seemed so long to him—so long!

Finally, after two weary hours, the woman came back, panting and glowing from the heat, but—she came alone, without Heidi. Strong Martin had gone up to the hay field above the rocks, with his whole family, early in the morning, and had remained there hard at work all day. None of them had seen Heidi since the day before.

Moreover, all along the way the woman had asked for her, here and there, but no trace of her was to be found.

At this the grandmamma, beside herself with fear and worry, broke into a loud lament.

"Oh, if only my son were here! Why did he have to go to the village today of all days? Heidi wouldn't have followed him! But she may have become homesick and tried to find her way back to her grandfather as she did when we had her with us in Frankfurt!"

"If she did, would not your son or some of the villagers in Wallis have seen her?" Kaspar's wife suggested.

"But where can we find people to inquire?" cried Frau Sesemann. "Kind woman, what shall we do?"

Kaspar's wife then offered to go to all the houses round about, and if no one had seen Heidi on the way to the village she would summon the people to start out on a searching party before it should be dark.

"I will summon a few and start out immediately," offered the doctor. "But where shall we search?"

The woman suggested that the searchers would have to go up along by the wild mountain brook and into the forest.

"If only they hadn't all gone up to make hay," she complained, but the doctor hurried off in the midst of her complaining. They were only wasting time discussing the matter when Heidi might, at that very moment, be trapped in some remote spot calling for help.

Klara, who now realized what might have happened to Heidi, began to weep bitterly.

"Oh, Grandmamma, it is my fault! She wanted me to go to the woods with her. She wanted me to see the red flowers and then, when you told the story about the burning bush, she wanted them more than ever! If she has fallen into the brook, which roars so frightfully, or if she went deep into the forest and lost her way, I am to blame!" she sobbed. "Oh, let us go right into the woods where the red flowers are! She must be there!"

"But Klärchen, you don't know where to find the flowers, and you are not strong—" began the grand-mamma.

"I am! I am!" cried Klara. "We must find Heidi, Grandmamma! Please let us go together and look for her. It will be better than just waiting."

These were also the grandmamma's thoughts. Klara took her hand and hurried up to the woods faster than she was able to go at ordinary times, for she hardly knew she was running, she was so anxious.

One hour after another passed. Many neighbor women had joined in the search. Children ran, searching and calling everywhere, but no trace of Heidi was discovered. Night came on.

Klara had been running in every direction through thickets and underbrush, until now she could run no more. But nowhere had she or any of the others who were searching seen any red flowers. Frau Sesemann, who had managed to keep up with her only by the greatest effort, stood breathless.

Finally the doctor came upon them and told them that the entire woods had been combed as far as the precipice above the foaming forest brook. To their questions he replied that he knew where the red flowers were and had looked there to find nothing but a maze of crisscrossing paths. Every path had been searched as well as the surrounding underbrush, and the men were agreed that it was useless to look there further.

With this discouraging news, he returned with them to the house where, first of all, he carried Klara up to her sleeping room and told her to remain perfectly quiet. The grandmamma, too, must rest. As soon as Heidi was found, the doctor promised to let them know.

In the meantime Herr Sesemann had returned from the village and, finding his own house empty, had gone over to the Martins' cottage where he heard, in a few words, what had happened. Martin was just coming to offer his help as he had heard from Kaspar's wife that a

They were determined to continue the search until Heidi was found

child was lost. He explained how, since early morning, he had been away with his wife and children, and that Heidi had not been seen by them.

Returning to Kaspar's cottage where a light was now shining from the window, Herr Sesemann talked it all over with the doctor, who feared Heidi might have wandered deep into the forest as far as the treacherous rocks. So Martin was asked to get together all the men in the neighborhood, provide them with good lanterns, and have some of them climb up to the high cliffs and hunt around everywhere and others go through the forest in every direction. Herr Sesemann and the doctor would join them, for they were determined to continue the search until Heidi was found.

Thus the men started off into the night, and Frau Sesemann heard one hour after another strike on the old wall clock downstairs, but the night passed away more slowly, more lingeringly than any she had watched through in all her life. She did not close her eyes. At every distant sound that fell on her ear she jumped up, forgetful of the doctor's orders, and said to herself:

"Now they are coming and bringing the child! But will she be alive or dead?"

But they did not come. From time to time Klara would come tiptoeing in softly.

"Are you asleep, Grandmamma?" she would whisper, for through her anxiety she could find no rest either. Then, discovering that her grandmamma was also awake, she would ask again and again, "Shall we not pray once more that the dear Lord will take care of Heidi and bring her home again soon?"

Frau Sesemann assented willingly each time, and then Klara would kneel down beside her bed and pray and beseech the dear Lord to protect Heidi from all harm.

"But Grandmamma," she protested tearfully when she had finished praying, "if the dear Lord has decided to take Heidi to Himself, how can our prayers change His mind?"

"That is a difficult question, Klärchen," admitted the grandmamma after thinking it over. "I hardly know the answer myself. But perhaps, when you are older, you will better understand the meaning of prayer. It is not like talking to a person, for God is a Spirit, so even when our prayers are not answered, they give us some comfort. Heidi herself could tell you that."

"Then, dear Lord, please be with the men who are searching for her," begged Klara, "and show them which way to go."

When she had prayed thus with the grandmamma, Klara went quietly back to her own room and finally fell asleep.

So the night passed. The beaming sun was already rising behind the mountains, lighting up the woods and meadows as if it had great joy to announce, when weariness at last overcame Frau Sesemann and she sank back exhausted on her pillow.

CHAPTER IV

The Next Morning

PALE AND WORRIED, Herr Sesemann came through the
golden morning light back to the house, and his clothes
showed plainly that he had pressed through many thorns
and prickly briers in the search. Behind him came the
doctor, who looked as if he were near collapsing. Frau
Sesemann had been awakened by the sound of their
footsteps and, full of anguish, called:

"Are you bringing the child?"

Her son came nearer, sat down by the bed, laid his
head in his hands and said, almost inaudibly:

"We come alone. Dear Mother, I can no longer hope,
no longer think. In what condition shall we find her after
the long night, wholly or half dead?"

"Oh, no, Papa," sobbed Klara, who had come in
softly, "the dear Lord has surely taken care of our Heidi,
for Grandmamma and I have prayed to Him so many
times in the night."

"You are right, Klara," said the doctor from the doorway. "Hold fast to your faith, and we may yet find her."
Turning to Herr Sesemann, he added, "We have gone
through the forest in every direction all night long. Now
we will go down through the ravine by the forest
brook."

The doctor spoke these words in a trembling voice.

The supposition that Heidi had fallen into the wild forest brook became more and more certain to him. Herr Sesemann had arranged for a good breakfast to be prepared for the men at Martin's house, and then they were all to help further in the search. Now that it was daylight, they would be better able to climb down into the ravines and gorges.

When Herr Sesemann and the doctor had finished their own breakfasts they returned to Martin's house to find the men still sitting at the table and talking excitedly about what to do next. Seppli was standing by his father, trying to make himself heard above the voices of the men.

"What is it that you want to say, little fellow?" the doctor asked kindly.

A silence ensued, for they all realized the boy had been trying to tell them something for some time. Suddenly he said bluntly:

"I know where she is."

"Don't talk such nonsense, Seppli," his father said reprovingly, and yet gently, too, for this was his way of speaking with his children. "You were up in the hay field when she was lost; you can't know anything about it."

Herr Sesemann had asked for ropes and other necessary things, and while these were being made ready Seppli edged over to the doctor and said half aloud but quite distinctly:

"But I really do know where she is."

"He might know something about it at that," the doctor said to the others. "He and Heidi were friends."

At this Herr Sesemann seized him by the hand, and said earnestly, "Little boy, look at me, and tell me truly, do you know anything about the lost child?"

"Yes," was the brief answer.

"Then speak out, boy! Have you seen her? Where has she gone?" asked the doctor with growing impatience.

"I will show you," replied Seppli, and went to the door.

They all rose. The men looked at one another skeptically. No one knew whether to take the suggestion seriously or as a foolish whim.

But the doctor followed the boy without any hesitation.

"Seppli, Seppli," said his father warningly, "I really think you are making a promise you can't keep."

But Seppli kept trotting along, the doctor following, and Herr Sesemann and the other men coming reluctantly after.

When the little fellow headed for the forest they stood still, and one of them said, "It is utterly useless to follow the boy in there, for we have searched through every place as far as the precipice and found nothing. We will not go."

Herr Sesemann thought, too, that it was useless. But something had to be done and he was willing to try it.

"What about you, my friend?" he asked the doctor.

"Give the boy a chance," was the good man's reply.

Martin informed them that he himself had little confidence in Seppli's ability to find Heidi. But the boy kept marching along and the three men decided to follow.

Seppli walked resolutely on, farther and farther into the woods. Suddenly he turned to the left towards the old fir trees where the searchers soon saw something red gleaming through the dark branches. Straight ahead, through the midst of briers and prickly thistles, Seppli steered them to another spot where there were many large bushes together, all covered with red flowers. Here he stood still and looked a little puzzled. He had evidently expected to find Heidi among the flowers. Then he went with determination on his way.

"It is no use, Seppli," said the doctor kindly. "We thought of the red flowers, too, and looked here yesterday when it was still daylight."

Without replying, the boy kept doggedly on.

The blossoming bushes became fewer, but larger and

larger. Seppli stood still by each one for a moment and looked around, then he would go on, always to the left.

"No, no, Seppli, don't go any farther," cried his father. "We are coming to the big wall of rock."

But at the same moment there was a shining like fire through the trees. The sun glowed on a bush completely covered with the red flowers. Seppli ran up to it quickly. He was close to the precipice which extended, rugged and steep, down to the deep ravine below.

"Seppli! Seppli! Take care!" called Strong Martin.

Always obedient to his father's commands, the boy walked more cautiously now. Grasping a branch for support, he looked around and across the flowers down over the rocks. Then he turned around. Herr Sesemann and the doctor exchanged hopeless glances. The path had come to an end, and Heidi was not found!

His father seized the boy by the hand and was about to pull him back from the dangerous spot, when Seppli said in his dry way:

"She is lying down there below."

The doctor rushed forward and peered over the precipice. His face grew deathly pale. He stepped back and had to cling to the nearest tree, his knees were shaking so. He beckoned to Martin, who was still holding Seppli fast by the hand, then to Herr Sesemann.

Both men stepped to the edge of the precipice and looked down. Here and there a few bushes hung over the steep wall of rock. Far below, the rock had one small projection, like a narrow shelf. Here lay, nestled on the moss-covered rock, a motionless little figure with her face pressed against the stone.

"God in Heaven, it is true, there she lies!" said Martin, shuddering, "but whether living or—"

He did not finish the sentence. One look at Herr Sesemann closed his lips. He was nearly as pale as the doctor. But he soon recovered himself.

"Martin," he said faintly, "no time is to be lost. If the

child moves she will be over the precipice. Who will climb down? Who will get her?"

The other men now came along with the ropes. Hopeless, they had followed their little guide through curiosity. They also looked, one after another, down the wall of rock.

"Listen, you men," said the doctor in a trembling voice. "Herr Sesemann is right. There is not a moment to lose. Who among you is experienced in this sort of thing? Speak up! You will be handsomely rewarded."

The men looked at one another, but all remained silent. One of them stepped to the edge, looked down, then turned around, shrugged his shoulders, and went away.

"If we were only sure that she is still alive," said another. "But a man risks his life and perhaps only to bring back a dead child."

"Who knows that she is not alive?" cried the doctor, almost beside himself, "and if she stirs she is lost beyond recovery! Oh, is it possible that none of you will go?"

"I wouldn't risk it," said one of the men, shaking his head.

"She would have been frightened and fallen down below long before this if she had been alive. No one could lie as still as that," said another. "And, sir, if one should roll down there, the best reward would be of no use."

"I will double it, even triple it!" cried Herr Sesemann.

But nothing would tempt the men to undertake the dangerous rescue. Shrugging their shoulders, one after another stepped back. There was no prospect of help.

"I will do it myself," the doctor suddenly spoke up. "Only show me how."

Martin stepped up to him.

"No, sir," he said quietly, "that will not do. You are so badly shaken up yourself that both would be lost. That is sure. But I will do it, with God's help. I have four little ones myself, and no one knows better than I how precious they are."

Even before he spoke he had fastened the big rope around the trunk of the old fir tree, for he had decided to bring up the little girl, whether she was dead or alive. Then he took off his cap, prayed softly, seized firm hold of the rope, and slid down the rock.

Finally he reached the little shelf in the rock. With one hand he held to the rope with all his strength, but he had to cling to the rock with his bare feet in order to grasp the child with his other hand and lift her up. Gently, quietly, he drew near, for if, by some miracle, she should be alive and should be startled by him—just a quick movement—even at the last moment she would be lost.

She lay motionless there. Martin bent over her and laid his broad, strong hand on her shoulder. At the same moment she was about to turn around quickly and would have fallen, but she was being held so firmly that she could only turn her head. A pair of big, wondering eyes looked up at the man.

"God be praised and thanked!" said Martin, taking a deep breath. "Say the same, little girl, if you can still speak!"

"Yes, I can speak! God be praised and thanked!" said Heidi in a clear voice.

Martin looked at her in the greatest amazement. She was wholly unharmed. It seemed to him that a miracle had taken place before his eyes.

"Can you put both your arms around my neck, very tight?" he asked gently. "You must do it yourself, for, you see, I cannot hold you. I have enough to do with both my hands, to climb up."

"Yes, yes, I will hold fast," Heidi assured him, and clasping Martin so firmly that he could hardly breathe, they began the difficult climb.

Above stood Herr Sesemann and the doctor with the men who had come along afterwards. They were watching, without drawing a breath, while Martin, the child still clinging to him, swayed in mid-air.

Nearer and nearer they came. Now only the last frightful, steep piece of rock! There, they were up! None of the men had ever seen such a daring rescue.

"God be thanked!" cried Martin, when he had taken the last step over the edge and stood on solid ground. He took Heidi from his neck and placed her in Herr Sesemann's arms.

"This child must be strangely dear to our Lord," Martin said reverently, "for He has worked a miracle for her."

"She is strangely dear to us," said Herr Sesemann in a husky voice. "Here, Doctor, take her! This is too much for me."

The doctor had been standing there as if in a daze. He was unable to speak.

"Oh, Doctor, I am so glad!" cried Heidi, throwing both arms around his neck. "I knew someone would surely find me in the morning."

Tears of joy now coursed down the doctor's cheeks and fell on Heidi's curly head. Martin stepped aside with folded hands. Seppli had pressed close to him and clung to him fast, for he realized that his father had been in great danger. Now Martin looked at the boy, frankly puzzled.

"Tell me, Seppli," he inquired in his gentle voice, "how did you know the little girl had come here?"

"Because she wanted to pick the red flowers," he replied.

"But what made you think she would be right there by the rock?"

"Because she was not by the first bush, so she must have gone farther, because the flowers keep getting more and more beautiful, and the most beautiful bush of all is the last near the rock. But I didn't know she had fallen over," explained Seppli.

CHAPTER V

Heidi's Gifts

DURING THE long trip back through the woods there was little conversation. But when they reached Kaspar's cottage, Herr Sesemann held out his hand to the rescuer.

"You know very well, Martin, how grateful I am to you for doing what I should have done myself," he said with deep sincerity. "I thank you as only one man can thank another to whom a life has been given back. Two lives, in fact, for my good friend, the doctor, would surely have lost his if he had undertaken to do what you, with God's help, succeeded in doing."

"We shall never forget that you risked your life for us," the doctor added. "How can we ever repay you?"

"It is reward enough that I was able to bring back the little girl unharmed," declared Martin.

"We will see about that, won't we, Heidi?" asked Herr Sesemann as they parted.

Inside the house Klara had awakened from a restless sleep to go in once more to pray with the grandmamma. She was still sitting by the bed and holding her hand while Frau Sesemann, quite exhausted, was lying back on her pillow with her eyes closed.

Herr Sesemann now stepped up to his mother's bed and placed Heidi in front of her while the doctor watched from the doorway.

"Good morning, Grandmamma! Did you sleep well?" said Heidi cheerfully, as she did every morning.

The grandmamma's eyes flew open.

"Am I still dreaming?" she exclaimed, staring at the child.

Klara was so astonished that, at first, she could not speak a word. She had not supposed her prayers would be answered in this unexpected fashion.

"Are you back again, Heidi?" she finally asked in a trembling voice. "What happened to you? Where were you all night long?"

Little by little, first Herr Sesemann and then the doctor told where they had found Heidi and how, after the doctor had offered to go down over the precipice himself, Strong Martin had risked his life to save her. The grandmamma shuddered at the description.

"Oh, weren't you frightened almost to death?" asked Klara, who, from sympathy, was trembling from head to foot.

Heidi thought it over for a moment before she answered:

"When I looked down I was, so I pressed my face close to the rock and didn't look. The stone where I landed was covered with moss, so I didn't hurt myself, and it was soft like my bed at home. But it was such a small stone that I had to push back tighter and tighter against the rock to keep from falling off before anyone could find me. Once I heard someone calling, but the voice was far away. When I answered, no one heard me, so I thought I would wait until whoever it was came a little nearer. But then I was tired and it was already dark, and I knew I might have to wait until morning."

"Oh, then you must have been frightened!" said Klara with a shudder. "Why did you go there, Heidi? Was it because of the red flowers?"

"Yes, I wanted to see them. I thought, if you could see them, you might go up in the woods with me," explained

Heidi. "The doctor said you could walk that far if you only thought so—"

"She did walk that far, and farther," the grandmamma put in quietly, "when we were looking for you."

"I'm glad, but I'm sorry I worried you so," Heidi added quickly. "At first I thought I would ask permission, but there was no one in the house, so I went for Seppli, but he was away, too. So then I thought I would find the red flowers alone, for Seppli had told me the way to go there."

"He knew the way all right," the doctor declared, "but go on, Heidi. Then what happened?"

"Then I went up into the woods and hunted a long, long time without finding the flowers," she continued her story. "I was about to go back home when suddenly I saw something red shining behind the trees and I ran towards it. At first there were only a few flowers and not very bright ones, but Seppli had said you had to go farther and farther into the woods. So I went still farther, and there were more and more flowers, and at last I came to a big, big bush with so many beautiful red flowers. It was a burning bush, exactly like the one Grandmamma told us about, only it was aflame with flowers. And there was an angel in it, too. I'm sure of it."

"There must have been," murmured the grandmamma. "A guardian angel!"

"It was the one on the sewing card," Heidi assured her. "She has such a beautiful face. And when I said the prayer underneath, it made me feel all quiet inside. So I went to sleep right after I had finished praying:

> *"Guardian Angel, hear me!*
> *On bright wings hover near me.*
> *God keep me from all harm!*
> *Through danger, fear, and sorrow,*
> *I'll sleep until the morrow,*
> *Protected by Thine arm.*

"And then," Heidi continued, "the strangest thing

happened. I felt someone's arm and I really thought, at first, that it was the arm of God. But it wasn't. It was Seppli's father."

"God may have been working through him," said the grandmamma thoughtfully.

"Of course," agreed Heidi. "He works through all of us if we let Him, doesn't He?"

"Indeed, He does," agreed the doctor, "even your little friend Seppli."

The grandmamma had not yet heard who had finally taken the searching party to the right spot, and wanted to know all about it. But Kaspar's wife had come in to announce that breakfast was ready so the story had to wait until everybody was seated around the table. Then it was explained that Seppli was really the first one to trace Heidi.

"We must especially reward the brave boy," Herr Sesemann finished, and Heidi, who grasped this idea with enthusiasm, immediately began to discuss it with Klara. What should the reward for Seppli be?

"He should, for once, have his greatest wish," said the doctor. "We must find out what will most delight his heart."

"Can I go and ask him right away?" Heidi questioned eagerly, jumping up from the table.

Herr Sesemann and the doctor decided to go with her to speak with Martin and also to recompense the other men.

Heidi, her breakfast finished, rushed out to where Seppli was standing, as usual, in front of his door gazing at the opposite house.

"Come, Seppli," she cried, "now you can have the very best thing you can think of!"

Seppli looked at Heidi as if her words had awakened something that lay heavy on his heart. Finally he said, quite cast down:

"It is of no use."

"Yes, really, it is," Heidi assured him. "Because you

found me you can ask for anything you would like, and
you shall have it. Herr Sesemann and the doctor are
agreed on it. Now think right away about it and then tell
me what it is."

Gradually Seppli seemed to understand the matter. He
looked at Heidi once more to see whether or not she was
really in earnest. Then he took a deep breath and said:

"A whip with a yellow lash."

Heidi was surprised at this modest wish.

"But Seppli, that is nothing!" she exclaimed. "You
must think of the most beautiful thing of all and wish for
that."

Seppli thought obediently, took another deep breath,
and said:

"A whip with a yellow lash."

Herr Sesemann then came out of Martin's house with
the men, who went away with many expressions of gratitude. But Martin himself remained in the doorway talking with the doctor.

"We have not yet given you any reward, Martin," he
was saying, "and to you, above any of the others, we
must prove our gratitude. Tell me, have you some special
desire?"

"Only name it and it shall be yours," put in Herr
Sesemann.

Martin turned his cap around for a while in his hands,
then said hesitatingly:

"I have had a great desire for a long time, but I dare
not tell you what it is; no, no, it should not have come
into my mind."

"Speak it out fully," said the doctor encouragingly.
"Perhaps we can help you."

"I have always thought," confessed Martin, "that if I
could only get on as well as my neighbor over there, I
would venture to think of buying a cow. I have quite a
good deal of hay and then could take care of my family
without anxiety."

"That is good, Martin," said Herr Sesemann, handing him the same amount of money he had given the others. "We shall see each other again."

Then the two men, with Heidi between them, started on the way back.

"And what did your friend Seppli wish for?" the doctor asked.

"He is a strange boy," replied Heidi. "He only wants a whip with a yellow lash."

It was not long before Herr Sesemann had to make another trip down into the valley. Heidi and Klara knew very well why. He had a long list of things to buy in the village. He did not go, however, without impressing it upon Heidi that she must not take a step away from the house without permission and that, if she did venture into the woods, she was to choose only the safe paths and that Klara and her grandmamma or the doctor were to go with her.

These warnings were entirely unnecessary as Heidi had her own plans. These included Klara, her grandmamma, and the large basket of knitting materials and sewing cards.

"If I sew one very carefully, may I take it home?" asked Heidi. "And may I choose any card I like?"

The grandmamma already suspected which card Heidi would choose. But she merely smiled and nodded. It seemed that Heidi and Klara had changed places for now it was Klara who was eager for a walk. She wanted to go up to the very spot where Heidi had fallen and give thanks from a full heart to the dear Lord who had, so evidently, sent His guardian angel to protect her friend. But Heidi had no desire to go back there. She spent the entire morning and most of the afternoon working industriously on the sewing card.

"It's my gift for the blind grandmother," she explained two days later when it was finished. "She told me to bring back myself, but I didn't know, until I fell over the precipice, how hard it would be, so now I'm giving her the picture of the angel and the prayer I said to keep up my courage until someone came."

Heidi's other gifts were all packed, among them the flowered cloth for Brigitte, a new pipe and tobacco for her grandfather, and now the finished sewing card. Only Peter's gift had still to be decided upon.

The journey back to Dörfli was to begin the following morning. After the farewells were all said, Heidi and the doctor started off on horseback while Klara looked wistfully after them.

"Next summer I will see you again, Heidi," she called, "and the summer after—"

"Yes, and the summer after that," Heidi called back.

And so they kept calling until their voices could no longer be heard.

Martin went with them to carry the bags while Seppli trotted along beside him until they had come to the end of the field path. There they stopped in amazement.

Fastened near the path stood a glossy brown cow, so big and splendid, such as was only seen occasionally among the rich peasants. To one of her horns was tied a big whip, which had a strong, white, leather mesh with a thick, silk lash which shimmered in the sun like gold!

A paper was bound around the whip handle and on this was written in large letters: "For Seppli."

When Martin had recovered from his astonishment and made sure that the cow was really his, he took down the whip and gave it to the boy.

"It is yours," he said.

Seppli held the whip in his hand as if he could not believe that the most wonderful thing he could think of was his very own! And, besides, there was the cow, which could be driven up on the mountain, with the whip to crack, like Georgie's and Chappi's! With beaming eyes, Seppli hugged his whip as if to say:

"No power on earth can take this away from me!"

Not until his father had reminded him, did he stop to

thank the doctor and Heidi, who had known all along that the cow would be tied there. Now they were waiting to see how it was received, and Heidi, above all, had to see what impression the whip would make as she had marked it for Seppli herself, and in the big traveling bag, all ready to be carried home, was another one exactly like it for Peter.

CHAPTER VI

How They Were Received

Now THE month of August was coming to an end. From the cloudless sky above the twin peaks of the Falkniss, the sun sent warm rays down on the grassy slope where, every day, Peter might be seen stretched on the ground before an open book while his goats nibbled the sweet grass around him.

Distelfink, curious at first, no longer poked an inquisitive nose between the pages. Schwänli and Bärli, too, watched from a respectful distance while Peter's own goat, Schnecke, and all the others went their own way as before. Their general, who for five years had been content to watch them and do nothing, was now far away in time and place, for the book he had chosen to read this morning was a textbook on ancient history.

The old schoolmaster had loaned Peter a whole stack of schoolbooks in the vain hope that he might at least glance at them during the summer. This year there would be a new schoolmistress and the previous teacher, whose constant ridicule had at first convinced Peter that it was impossible to learn anything, did not want to turn his scholars over to her entirely untaught.

Peter had Heidi to thank for the fact that he had finally learned to read. She was the only true friend he had, for he took no pleasure in the companionship of other boys and when, during recess, they thrashed each other, or played at wrestling, or divided themselves into teams for mock battles, he went away without even looking back at them. If they called out after him, "Now it is Peter's turn to be thrashed," he stood perfectly still and did nothing; but he looked at them so fiercely that no one bothered him.

In Heidi's company he was always contented. Since she had come to school things had changed somewhat and would change still more, Peter now felt certain, if he knew his lessons well. He took such pleasure in planning this surprise for her that the day in the pasture fairly flew. Almost before he knew it the sky began to glow like fiery gold. Peter closed his book, stood up and began to sing at the top of his voice:

> *"Little lambkins, come down*
> *From the bright, sunny height;*
> *The daylight is fading,*
> *The sun says, 'Good night!'"*

"You should be singing, 'Little goats!'" cried a voice almost in Peter's ear as the goats came leaping over the golden rocks which were already glowing from the fiery sunset. Down they came, one after the other, from the green Alp above. Soon Heidi was surrounded by them. Peter was so surprised to see her that he did nothing at first. He could only stand still and stare.

"I'm home again," announced Heidi, her black eyes sparkling with pleasure at the sight of Peter and his goats all looking as if they were gilded in the evening sunlight. "Here, take this!" she added, handing him the whip in its paper package. "It's the present I brought you from the Gemmi."

Quickly Peter undid the wrappings, looked briefly at the whip, laid it inside his book to mark the place, and then took Heidi's hand.

"Come," he said. "We will go down together."

They walked like this for a little while in silence drinking deep of the beauty that surrounded them.

"Nothing was like this on the Gemmi," said Heidi softly. "The snow-capped mountains and green woods with the blazing red flowers were beautiful, but nothing like this. I'll always come back here. Sometimes I wonder if it can be any more beautiful in heaven where all the blessed are rejoicing."

"Why are they rejoicing?" Peter wanted to know.

"Oh, because they are free from all sorrow and pain," replied Heidi, "and because the blind can see how beautiful it all is behind the sunset. Your grandmother told me."

"Is that where they are?" asked Peter skeptically.

"Oh, Peter!" said Heidi with some impatience. "Must you always *know?* I like to *think* it is. If the dear Lord lights up His dwelling place so beautifully from the outside, can't you just *believe* it is even more beautiful within?"

Peter acknowledged this. It sounded reasonable. But still he paid no attention to his whip. Finally Heidi asked:

"Don't you like your present, Peter? You only need to crack a beautiful whip like that to send your goats in the right direction. This way!"

And Heidi took the whip and gave it such a tremendous crack that the goats leaped ahead of them along the path as if a storm had broken loose behind them.

"See!" cried Heidi triumphantly. "You'll never have to beat them."

But Peter was looking at the book in his hand.

"You've lost my place," he said briefly.

Now it was Heidi who stared. She had brought him a whip, thinking he would have no use for a book. What had come over him? He was not like the old Peter at all.

"Seppli liked his whip," said Heidi. "The last I saw of

him he was standing there hugging it as if it were the most precious thing in the whole world."

"Who is Seppli?" Peter immediately demanded.

"A boy I met on the Gemmi. His father is Strong Martin, who rescued me when I fell, so the doctor bought him a brown cow, and I gave Seppli a whip like yours because he was the one to show his father where I was."

This explanation aroused Peter. When Heidi had told him all about it, he scowled so darkly that one might easily have believed it frightened all the splendor away. At any rate the sky darkened, too, as Peter growled, "I hate this boy, Seppli. He is my enemy."

"Why do you say that?" cried Heidi. "You don't even know him! You are acting exactly as you did with Klara when you pushed her rolling chair down the mountain. You don't even like it when I make friends in school."

This was true, as Peter knew very well. The book he had been reading must have had a solemn effect on him, for he looked at Heidi soberly and replied, in all earnest:

"You see, Heidi, you don't know in the least what friendship is, for you believe you can have a different friend every week. You should have only one friend for your whole life, and his enemy would have to be dragged along the wall of Troy three times and made to suffer."

"So that is what you think!" retorted Heidi with flashing eyes. "If you get such ideas from reading books you are better off with a whip!"

At this Peter threw down the whip as if it had stung him and raced off down the mountain. But it was only Heidi's words that had stung. She was immediately sorry and ran after him, calling:

"I didn't mean it! I didn't mean it! I want you to read. Really, I do. But wait for me, Peter! I have another gift for your mother and still another for your grandmother, and my grandfather said you were to go with me to help me carry them!"

Peter halted suddenly. He had great respect for the Alm Uncle and his orders. Heidi was breathless when she caught up with him. The whip he had thrown away was in her hand.

"Take it! Take it!" she panted. "It's yours, Peter; I want you to have it, but you must understand that

whoever is my friend doesn't need to be your enemy. You should make new friends, too. Why don't you, Peter? Why don't you sing in school the way you were singing to the goats up there on the mountain?"

"I can't," said Peter, accepting the whip. "They think I'm stupid."

"They won't this year," Heidi assured him. "There will be a new teacher, and when all the children sing you will join in and sing with them. And, Peter, if you've studied your books, it will be even better. I don't much care that you didn't want your whip."

"But I do want it," declared Peter. "It's a splendid whip. Now are we friends?"

"Always," said Heidi. "You may have my hand on it. Now you know it is true, for whatever is promised with the hand can never be taken back."

These words were followed with a solemn handclasp which made Peter's face light up with pleasure, for now he had a friend for all time, whatever should happen.

"But I don't want to be your only friend," Heidi continued. "I meant what I said about making new friends in school."

Peter pondered over this, for the thought of having any friend except Heidi had never occurred to him. Now, however, they were near the Alm hut. The grandfather had been watching what was going on above him with some amusement. He stopped puffing on the new pipe Heidi had given him and said slyly:

"So Heidi and the Goat General have a solemn pact."

"It's a pact of friendship, Grandfather," explained Heidi. "We're always going to be friends, no matter what happens, and I'm always going to come back here, wherever I go. It's so beautiful here on the Alm."

"And what do you think of it?" asked the Alm Uncle, turning to the silent Peter.

"Oh, I like it fine," replied the boy. "I don't believe it could be more beautiful anywhere."

"Neither do I," agreed the grandfather, full of satisfaction. "You think just what I think. I'd like to know where it could be finer. Where do they have such golden sunshine as we have up here or such pure air which simply fills one with health? Everyone can breathe as much of it, too, as he can hold. And what strength this air and sunshine give! I tell you I know something about it. I was not always as happy as I am now. Of course when I was young like you I was happy, for I had a mother and father who watched over me and a very dear brother. But I was restless and had bad comrades who persuaded me to leave home against the wishes of my family. We traveled far, at first as workmen and later as soldiers. It was an adventurous life, but not a good one. Finally, after an unhappy, extravagant marriage, I became so homesick that I had to return."

"With my father?" asked Heidi, who had been listening attentively to the grandfather's words.

"Yes, the boy Tobias was with me. But what did we find? Both father and mother were dead and the brother, Henrico, had gone away, nobody knew where.

" 'It wouldn't have happened so if you had stayed at home,' our neighbors said. And you can believe me, these words burned deeply into my soul. They told me it was the judgment of the Lord when other troubles came, so I turned against Him and could find no peace until I came up here where it is so open that one can look about in all directions and it is hard to keep the thoughts from striving upwards. So it was when you came to me, Heidi, and brought the Lord's blessing on my humble hut."

"Amen," said Peter as if he were in church.

The Alm Uncle's words had made a solemn impression on Heidi, too, as she had always wanted to know more about her grandfather's solitary existence before she came to live with him.

"What are you two thinking about so earnestly?" asked the old man after a considerable silence.

"I would like to know what became of your brother, Henrico," replied Peter. "The villagers often speak of him."

"Did you ever try to find him, Grandfather?" asked Heidi.

"It is of no use," he replied, rising from his seat, "but now I have talked about myself long enough. Peter must go along with his goats and you with your presents." With twinkling eyes, he added, "I hope the grandmother can see her picture."

When they were on their way, with the big bolt of cloth slung over Peter's back, he turned to Heidi, skipping along beside him and holding her square package high to keep it from being nibbled by the frisking goats.

"What sort of a picture is it?" he asked. "How can the grandmother see it when she is blind?"

"She will," Heidi promised and skipped happily on until they had reached the little wooden house in the hollow halfway down the Alm.

Peter stopped only long enough to see how Heidi's presents were received. A picture that the grandmother could see still seemed unbelievable, and he was curious. But first he placed the big bolt of cloth on the table and helped his mother unroll it.

"Beautiful, Heidi! Beautiful!" exclaimed Brigitte when she had taken a long look at the rich flowered material. "Now I shall dress up this old house like a mansion. Perhaps I could take someone to board for the rest of the season. You know sometimes invalid ladies or delicate children come from the city to the country, and I could take good care of them."

"I'm sure you could," replied Heidi, a little puzzled at this unexpected turn of events. Brigette went on explaining how she could make new curtains for the windows and cover the old furniture.

"Is that the child?" called the grandmother from the next room. "Is that our Heidi's voice?"

"It is, Grandmother! I have brought back myself, and here is my guardian angel!"

And, with this, Heidi thrust the picture she had embroidered on the sewing card into the grandmother's wrinkled hands and told her to feel the little stitches all around the edge and around the angel's face and the little, short stitches that outlined each one of her curls and each feather on her spreading white wings.

"I see! I see!" murmured the grandmother over and over as her fingers moved searchingly over the picture. Peter stood watching for a moment. Then he waved his cap to Heidi to show he understood, and went out, cracking his whip until it startled the poor grandmother, and she gasped:

"What is it, Heidi? What is it? Is the house really falling to pieces at last?"

"No, no, nothing of the kind," Heidi reassured her. "It is only Peter with his new whip. Now you can hear him singing!"

"And the lambkins! And the lambkins!" sounded above the cracking of the whip.

"Peterli has a good voice," said the grandmother with satisfaction. "He should use it more often."

"He does, up in the pastures," declared Heidi, "and he has promised me that now he will take part in the singing in school. And Grandmother, he reads whole books!"

"Yes, yes, child. All about wars and fighting. He has read some to me, and I like the old hymns better."

"Then listen to what it says underneath the angel in your picture!" cried Heidi. "It isn't a hymn. It's a prayer to say at night when—when you're afraid or—or anything."

And, holding her folded hands over the grandmother's wrinkled ones, Heidi began to read the prayer:

> *"Guardian Angel, hear me!*
> *On bright wings hover near me."*

But here she had to stop reading. The memory of that dreadful night on the precipice and the thought of what could have happened quite overcame her. But the grandmother supposed she had finished, and said, very low:

"May she always be with you, Heidi."

"And with you, Grandmother," Heidi whispered.

"Yes, yes, child!" the grandmother assured her. "I shall keep her on this little table within reach of my chair so that I can take her out and look at her whenever I feel like it. Really, I can see her quite well with my fingers. She is very much like you with her curly hair."

CHAPTER VII

In the High Pastures

A BEAUTIFUL, warm September sun was shining outside over the green hills around Dörfli. A few beams fell through the opaque windowpanes on the grandmother's bed.

"Ah, me!" she sighed, "is the sun still shining? If only I could go outside and feel the warm rays on my back. I could better stand the cold winter ahead."

"You mustn't worry about the winter yet," said Brigitte soothingly. "Our Lord will still be alive then; He has helped us many times, when things looked bad. What do you say if we make a little drop of coffee to warm you up?"

The grandmother was glad to drink a little cup of coffee, and glad, too, that Heidi had arrived to accompany Peter to the high pastures. Only a few days remained before school would begin and the two were eager to be off on another day's adventure.

Brigitte beckoned Heidi to come in, and immediately Peter followed, for he had to see what was going to be prepared to eat. His mother took down the pot from its place on the shelf and poured water into it. Then she said, "Heidi, would you like to help? What do you do first?"

"First I must grind the coffee beans," said the child and

immediately sat down with the old coffee mill on the stool and turned it with all her might. But there was something wrong with it, and she examined it first one way and then another, and finally drew out the little drawer to find out the trouble. Instead of the fine powder she ought to have seen, there were big pieces of almost half coffee beans. Heidi, in horror, held out the drawer to Peter, who tried to keep her quiet.

"You mustn't let the grandmother hear or she will be troubled and think she can't have any more coffee to drink. Just wait!"

Whereupon Peter went out and soon came back with a big stone in his hand. With this he broke and crushed the coffee beans on a paper, and then Heidi shook the coarse powder into the pot. But when the blind grandmother took the cup in her hand and drank a little, she exclaimed pitifully, "Oh dear! Oh dear! Big grains are floating on the top. The coffee mill is broken and we are not able to buy a new one."

"We shall be soon," replied Brigitte, who seemed to have some secret plan in her head. "Now drink what you can. Later you may feel strong enough to sit outside while I clean the rooms."

Heidi and Peter each had a little cup of coffee and brown bread to go with it. Then they packed a small lunch of bread and cheese and hurried on up the mountainside with the goats frisking and skipping ahead of them. Occasionally Peter would crack the whip Heidi had given him. This seemed to frighten the goats and make them hurry all the faster. Heidi and Peter had to run to keep up with them. They arrived at the Alm hut pink-cheeked and out of breath.

Here Heidi had to stop a little, but Peter planted himself immediately in front of the Alm Uncle, who was sitting on the wind-sheltered bench in the sunshine.

"What is it, Goat General? Why are you in such a hurry?" Heidi's grandfather asked calmly.

"I am late. I meant to be here much sooner," replied

Peter, having at last gained his breath. "Where are Schwänli and Bärli?"

"There they are!" cried Heidi, pointing up the grassy slope where the grandfather's goats had already joined the rest of the herd.

Now they all skipped and jumped ahead of the children as if in a great hurry to get to the high pasture where the grass was still dotted with sweet-smelling flowers.

"We shall go higher than ever before," announced Peter. "We shall go to the very top of the slope where we can look down on the other side!"

"Is it very far?" asked Heidi, who could not understand Peter's sudden ambition to reach the top.

"We should be there by noon," was his short reply.

Heidi hurried after him. The whip in his hand cracked in the morning air and sent the goats on ahead, higher and higher. In the spring these high pastures were covered with snow, but now the warm September sun had melted it all and sent it rushing down in rivulets to the valley below. Not a house was to be seen on all the green hills around, except on the Alm where a steep footpath went down to Dörfli and continued as a winding road as far as Maienfeld.

"How tiny the houses seem from up here!" exclaimed Heidi, looking back.

Peter did not answer. Something seemed to be driving him ahead. Was it something he wanted to see? Heidi thought of the blind grandmother, who could only sit in the sunshine and never see anything except with her fingers. She thought of the Gemmi and the guardian angel who had kept her from falling off the precipice. She thought of the grandfather, who would worry if they went too far.

Usually it was Heidi who wanted to rush ahead and Peter who held back. But the books he had been reading had changed him into an adventurer and Heidi had to follow, even when she would have liked to stop and look at the strange fields through which they were passing.

"I will not go on. I am too hot," Heidi said at last and sat down on the ground.

"No, Heidi, come. We are nearly to the top," commanded Peter. "Stand up and come quickly."

Heidi remained obstinately sitting on the ground. But Peter gave her no rest. He took her by the hand and pulled her up.

"You must come, Heidi. We have only to cross a swinging bridge across the glacier brook and then we come to the chapel."

"The chapel!" exclaimed Heidi in utter surprise. "What kind of a chapel, Peter? Did you dream about it?"

"No, Father Klemens told me. He says if we go into the chapel to pray, the Lord sends us something. We could go in and say the Lord's Prayer. The goats have stopped to graze on the meadow just below. They will be safe until we come out."

"But is the chapel very far?" Heidi protested.

"Just climb a little more and you will see it," Peter urged her on.

It was true. There, at the very top of the slope, stood a lonely chapel, looking down on the rushing water from the glacier brook. The bridge that crossed over to it was so narrow that only one person at a time could go over it. Peter went first. Heidi followed, glad for the railing on both sides, for the bridge was so lightly built that it trembled and swayed with every step she took.

When she was across she followed Peter into the dim chapel, and both of them repeated their prayer very reverently for they were truly thankful they had reached it in safety. After some time, when they had come out again, they heard voices and a heavy panting sounded from a footpath which descended to the other side.

Then, one after another, three heads came in sight, first a little girl's head, and then two boys' heads, and then all at once three children stood before Peter and Heidi and they all looked at one another with mutual astonishment.

The little girl who had first appeared was the largest of them all. She must have been quite eleven years old and the larger of the brothers about a year younger, or near Heidi's age. The second brother was considerably smaller. He stood in front of the other two and said, "Hello, what are your names?"

Peter and Heidi told him.

"Where is your home?" asked the child, further.

"In Dörfli, there. You can see it from the top of the slope," replied Heidi. "Where do you live?"

"In Nolla," the boy began, but his sister interrupted. "No, Karl. We used to live there, but now we live with our grandparents in one of those houses down below."

"It's the little one under the big willows," explained the older boy, who said his name was Kurt. He introduced his sister as Lissa and the little brother as Karl and said they were the grandchildren of the basketmaker, Willow Joseph. Their father had left them there when he went to look for work and told them they could earn their keep delivering the baskets their grandfather made.

"Do you deliver them in Dörfli?" asked Peter.

"No, only in Liezensteig," the children replied. "There it is, on a slope of the Falkniss. It is a long climb up to the dairyman's where we deliver the baskets. We always stop at the chapel to rest and pray for our father's return."

"I'll pray for him, too," Heidi promised impulsively. Her heart always went out to anyone in trouble so that keeping all her promises to pray for people sometimes made her prayers very long.

"Will you pray in church?" little Karl wanted to know.

"Yes, and at home, too. Our church is not like your chapel," Heidi explained. "It is closed during the week. We only go on Sunday."

"We come up here any day. There's another chapel higher up. See it, way up on top of the mountain."

The girl pointed with her finger, and her brothers nodded to show that they agreed with their sister that such chapels were very necessary.

"But why do you have them way up here?" asked Heidi.

"So that you can go in and pray when you pass by," Lissa answered quickly.

"You can do that anyway," said Heidi, still puzzled. "You can pray anywhere, wherever you are, for the dear Lord hears us everywhere, that I know."

"Yes, but you don't think of praying until you come to the chapel," replied Lissa earnestly.

"Now we must go, Heidi," urged Peter, for these ideas were too profound for him.

But Heidi was in no hurry. She enjoyed making new friends and Lissa pleased her because she made such decided answers and had just said what Heidi could not deny. She and Peter had never stopped to pray before although she had just said decidedly to Lissa that you could pray anywhere. Now she realized that this ancient chapel was a reminder. It was as if the dear Lord pointed down from Heaven and said, "There it stands, so that you may think of Me."

As Heidi, absorbed in thought, did not speak for a long time, Lissa continued, "And it is not like a command, but rather a favor that we may go in and pray, for the dear Lord always sends us something, although we cannot always see it right away."

"I would rather have something I can see right away," spoke up little Karl, and Kurt added, "Yes, something like the money Father Klemens gives us for our baskets."

"So would I," agreed Peter. "Does he fill them with provisions for the needy?"

"Yes, he does. Do you know Father Klemens, too?" asked Lissa.

She seemed delighted when Peter nodded and said he

did. The kind Father was well known to all the children on the other side of the brook for a long distance, and was their good friend, just as the pastor in Dörfli was to Heidi. Lissa explained it very well. Whenever he was seen in his long cloak, the big crucifix hanging at his side, children would run to him from every direction, and he would immediately take out his old pocketbook from under his full robe and give a lovely, bright-colored picture to each one.

"That is something you can see," continued practical Kurt. "Lissa has received many of them, with rosy angels, scattering flowers, and others with a bush full of blooming roses, and a little bird sitting on the very top. He lives up in the old monastery, and he often comes to see us."

"Sometimes he brings us a whole loaf of bread," added little Karl, in whose memory this fact stood out clearly.

"He visits the blind. That is how I met him," explained Peter. "He brought bread to my grandmother in one of your baskets. She has bread now, but no coffee and no money to buy a new coffee mill."

"That is too bad," all three children agreed.

They stood there a moment in silence, sympathizing with each other, and then Heidi said warmly, "Will you come to see us sometime in Dörfli?"

She wanted to continue the new acquaintance, but Lissa hesitated, saying, "I don't know the way."

"It is very easy to find. Come early some Sunday afternoon," said Heidi encouragingly. "Then we can play with the pastor's children. Sally is about your age and there are two boys, Max and Bruno, to play with your two brothers. You have only to go along the footpath, up to the top of the slope and then down and down, and there is Dörfli. The first big house you come to is the doctor's house where Grandfather and I spend the winter. You will know it at once by the walled garden. The parsonage and the church with the tall steeple are just below it."

"You have to pass my house," Peter put in, "so stop first a little higher up on the slope. On the very highest ground is the hut of the Alm Uncle, Heidi's grandfather, and that is where we are going now. So come, then!"

With this the children parted, and Peter was telling Heidi they would probably never see them again when suddenly there came something tumbling down the hill that caused Heidi to start back in surprise and Peter to stand stock still and stare upward with wide open eyes. It was a big flock of sheep, old and young. All were swarming, hopping and jumping together, and beside them the big sheep dog ran barking emphatically to prevent any from being lost.

"Oh, look at the lambkins!" exclaimed Heidi when she had recovered her breath, for they immediately made her think of their song.

The shepherd drove his flock past the children towards Dörfli, but still Heidi could not take in enough of the merry gambols which the young lambs made beside their mothers or the great care with which the older sheep looked after them.

When the flock had almost passed out of sight Heidi, still lost in astonishment, drew a long breath and said, "Now we must sing about them. Let's try it. Let's sing together:

> *"Little lambkins, come down*
> *From the bright, sunny height—"*

Here Peter joined in, and they finished the first verse together and began on the chorus:

> *"And the lambkins, and the lambkins,*
> *And the heavens so blue;*
> *And the red and white flowers,*
> *And the green grasses, too."*

Heidi was quite excited as she skipped along beside him. Now she paused, thought a bit, looked up and then down, and sang again:

"Little lambkins, above
On the bright, pleasant hill;
The sunlight is sparkling,
The winds are not still."

"Neither are you," declared Peter as she ran ahead of him and bounded so high over the lightly built bridge that it tottered and trembled under her feet. Behind her followed Peter watching to make sure she came safely to the other side.

Now they began at the very beginning, and sang the whole thing through again, and made merry over it, and were so happy that they sang it at least ten times over while Peter cracked his whip in time to their singing; and the more they repeated it, the better it sounded to their ears.

Meanwhile the goats had scattered. By the time Peter had rounded them up and Heidi had counted every last one to make sure all were there, the sun was low in the sky and already the tops of the mountains were beginning to glow with its fading rays. It was another hour before the children came with the goats to the last slope, still singing merrily:

"Little lambkins, come down
From the bright, sunny height;
The daylight is fading,
The sun says, 'Good night!'"

CHAPTER VIII

In Dörfli

For more than an hour Heidi's godfather, the doctor, had walked anxiously back and forth, first from the front room out on the stone steps of the house, then down into the street, looked around and then turned back, and after a little while, took the same walk over again.

"What is it, my friend? What is troubling you?" asked the pastor, coming out of his house next door and beginning to walk with the doctor.

"It is Heidi," the good man replied. "Can it be she is staying with the grandfather? But tomorrow is school and she is eager to go. Is it true that your sister will be the new teacher?"

"Quite true," agreed the pastor. But now he, too, was worried. It had grown quite dark and still not a sound from either Heidi or Peter was to be heard anywhere. What could have happened to them? The goats should have been returned to their owners long before this.

Every possible anxiety arose in the mind of the pastor's wife when she was told that Heidi had not returned. She questioned her children, first Sally, as she and Heidi had become good friends; then Max, a year older than his sister, and finally six-year-old Bruno. Each child replied in turn that he had not seen Heidi and could not understand why she would stay away when she and the doctor had both been invited for supper.

But what was that? Outside there was the sound of singing mixed with the bleating of goats and the cracking of a whip. The sound came nearer and soon Heidi ran in by herself, having left Peter to return the innkeeper's goats. She began at once an excited, if somewhat incoherent account of what had happened. It was interrupted by a loud voice from the kitchen:

"Come to supper! Come to supper!"

It was Lisebeth, who had cooked meals for the young pastor and his father before him. She seemed cross with Heidi and kept muttering to herself as she served her. The others, all seated around the table, were waiting to hear Heidi's story. But now it was not so easy to tell. First she had to explain Peter's desire to go into the chapel and pray for a new coffee mill.

"Did he think it would fall like manna from Heaven?" asked the pastor with a chuckle.

Finally it came out that the children had crossed the wild glacier brook. Heidi had such a pleasant memory of the swaying and trembling of the swinging bridge that she described it very vividly. Then she was questioned further by the doctor and the whole story came out in full force; first about the chapel, then the three children from Nolla, then the flock of sheep, and afterwards everything all over again from the beginning and in still greater detail.

"If only we had a little lamb like the lambkins you saw, Heidi, I would be perfectly happy," Sally said when the story was finished.

She repeated this wish the following morning when Heidi and Peter met her and the two boys, Max and Bruno, on their way to school.

"Where would you keep it, in the church?" asked Peter a little crossly.

Heidi was so amused by the picture his question brought before her eyes that she began to laugh and the others joined in until Peter found himself laughing, too.

Now, however, they were near the schoolhouse, and a troop of noisy children came towards them from the opposite direction. They all entered together, and soon the new teacher came in.

She was a pleasant-looking woman with light hair and a round, happy face. Heidi was delighted. She leaned over and whispered to Sally, "Why, she looks just like your Aunt Meili."

"She *is* my Aunt Meili."

Sally spoke louder than she meant to, and several of the children laughed. The teacher rapped for attention and began, immediately, to call the roll.

"You are all graded here," she observed, "but I shall not decide on that until I have seen what you can do."

Peter, sitting towards the back of the schoolroom with the big boys, looked a little uncomfortable when he heard this, but Heidi smiled to reassure him. She had great faith in Peter's ability. Now all he needed was a little faith in himself.

A busy morning of spelling and pronouncing followed. Then came the multiplication table which Peter knew by heart, and, lastly, the singing. For this the teacher brought out a shining violin and tuned it. Then she tucked it under her chin and began to play, letting the children choose the song. All shouted at the top of their lungs:

"Little lambkins, come down
From the bright, sunny height—"

until they had sung all the verses they knew, but the teacher taught them still more:

"And the lambkins, and the lambkins,
They jumped up so high;
And all were most merry,
And did not know why."

Heidi, however, had her eyes fixed so attentively upon

the violin and on the teacher's fingers as she touched the strings, that she forgot to sing, but turned around and whispered one word to Peter:

"Watch!"

At this Peter, too, became silent and the whole choir lost their pitch, and fell away a half note, and the violin became uncertain, and lost a half note also. Then the voices fell lower still, until at last nobody could have told what they were trying to sing.

"What sort of a song do you call that?" cried the teacher, putting down the instrument. "You are nothing but a lot of screamers! I should like to know who has put us all off key."

At this Heidi raised her hand.

"I know why it all went wrong," she explained. "It went that way because Peter stopped singing."

Now the teacher herself could see that the violin was somewhat dependent on Peter's leading, and told him so. After this the boy sang with his steady, clear voice; the violin followed, and the children sang with all their might; and so the first day of school went on quite satisfactorily to the very end.

Outside the schoolhouse Heidi and Peter freed themselves from the crowd of children gathering around them and wandered off together.

"What were you trying to tell me today when we were singing?" asked Peter. "I could not hear you in the back of the room. Were you thinking about yesterday?"

"No, it was quite another thing," replied Heidi. "I know how to play 'Little Lambkins' if I only had a violin."

A deep sigh accompanied these words as the wish was very dear to Heidi's heart. Understanding this, Peter at once began to contrive some means of helping her wish to come true.

"Perhaps we can make a violin," he said consolingly. "It is nothing but a bit of wood with four strings stretched across it. Do you think the teacher would lend us hers for a copy? You must ask her about it tomorrow morning."

So it was settled, but Heidi resolved to take the matter first to Sally, who might have more influence with her aunt. Peter had made plenty of whistles out of hollow elder branches but, somehow, she doubted his ability to make a violin.

After school the next day Heidi waited for Sally, but all Sally could think about was the little lamb she wanted. It didn't matter to her at all that Heidi's heart was set on possessing a violin. They were such a long time in conversation that Peter became quite overcome with impatience and dashed up to Heidi the moment she and Sally had parted.

"What did she say? Will the teacher lend us her violin?"

"I don't know," Heidi admitted. "Sally didn't give me a chance to ask."

"Never mind; you can try again tomorrow," Peter said cheerfully, taking her by the hand and walking her the rest of the way home.

The same thing happened the next day and the day after. Heidi called for Sally and listened to her chatter without once getting in a word about the violin. On Friday, however, as Heidi was standing timidly before the door of the parsonage, it opened suddenly, and the teacher came out quickly and ran into Heidi with such force that the child was thrown backwards into a rose bush.

"What is it, Heidi? Are you hurt? Why do you stand before the door without knocking?" asked the teacher in surprise and some displeasure. "Are you calling for my niece or do you wish to tell me something?"

"Could I—could we—I mean could Peter and I borrow your violin?" Heidi blurted out the question in thoughtless haste. The teacher's surprise and displeasure increased visibly.

Drawing the bow across the strings, she played several notes firmly and with spirit

"I do not understand," she said with a severe glance at Heidi's flushed face. "Have you come here on purpose to mock me? Of course I would not let a child borrow my violin. Now I will tell you what a violin costs, and then you will see how foolish you are. Six hard *Gulden* I paid for mine. Can you realize what that means?"

"But—but I know I could play it," stammered Heidi.

"It cost six *Gulden*," the teacher repeated. "We will separate it into *Blutsgers*. If one *Gulden* contains a hundred *Blutsgers*, then six *Gulden* will equal six times one hundred—quickly, quickly! Now, Heidi, you are generally ready enough."

"Six hundred *Blutsgers*," said the child softly.

"Moreover," continued the teacher, "do you imagine you have only to take a violin in your hand to be able to play on it at once? It takes a long time to do that. Come inside for a moment." And the teacher opened the door of her own sitting room and took the violin from its case. "There," she said as she placed it on Heidi's arm, "take the bow in your hand—so, and if you can play me one note correctly I will let you come here and practice."

"You will?"

Heidi could hardly believe her good fortune. The sad, sweet music of the violin reminded her of the wind in the fir trees and a great desire arose in her to learn to play it. She held the instrument exactly as the teacher had done while her eyes sparkled with the fire of her ambition. Drawing the bow across the strings, she played several notes firmly and with spirit.

Hearing her, Sally burst in and exclaimed, "You are playing 'Little Lambkins'! Where did you learn the violin, Heidi? Who taught you? How do you find the notes?"

"How, indeed?" asked the teacher, unable to conceal her admiration. "Now answer me truly and honestly. How did you learn to play this air so correctly?"

Looking up with sparkling eyes, Heidi replied, "I

learned it from you in school when the children were singing. I watched very carefully and did everything just the same."

"Then come tomorrow for your first lesson. I am a woman of my word," declared the teacher, now with unconcealed admiration, "but now I must hurry along or the children will all be in school ahead of me."

"We will walk more slowly. There is plenty of time for us," declared Sally, taking Heidi's hand.

The two would have walked together, but now Peter appeared from where he had concealed himself behind the woodpile at the side of the parsonage.

"You kept me waiting a long time. I have two good boards and a saw. Have you asked the question?"

"It is no use, Peter," Heidi replied. "You could not make a violin. If you would hold one, just once, you would know it for yourself. They are made by experts, and just think! The teacher's violin cost six hundred *Blutsgers*. I can never buy one, but she did say she would give me lessons on her violin."

"Lessons!" sniffed Peter. "What good are lessons if you have no instrument of your own?"

"Heidi did play 'Little Lambkins'—just the beginning," Sally explained, "but I knew what it was and told her so. She wants a violin and I want a lamb, and you, Peter, want a coffee mill for your grandmother, but we can never have them."

"Never, never," Peter agreed.

Only Heidi had faith that somehow, someway, all their deepest desires would be fulfilled.

CHAPTER IX

The Day of the Violin Lesson

WHEN HEIDI AWOKE the following morning, she was conscious of an unusual light-heartedness, and at first she thought she must be still on the Alm with the grandfather. Then she remembered that he had decided to remain with his goats a little longer and she had come to Dörfli to live with her godfather in the manor house they called their winter quarters and go to school. The thought of school reminded her of the teacher, and that she had said, on the previous morning, "Come tomorrow for your first lesson."

The violin, then, was the cause of it. Heidi could hardly eat her breakfast, she was so excited. When it was finished and all the dishes taken away, she began to wash the table. But the doctor said, "Now you may go along, my child. Lisebeth is coming in to take care of the housework, and if you start early there will be time for you to meet Peter."

"Oh, thank you! Thank you!" cried Heidi, and away she flew like a bird whose cage door has suddenly been opened.

An hour later both Heidi and Peter appeared in school, but the events that had transpired during that hour left them both a little bewildered. Sally became curious, but she had no chance to ask Heidi about it until the bell sounded for dismissal in the afternoon.

In a short time the schoolhouse door was opened and the flock hurried out into the open square where all at once they seemed to crowd into a big throng, from the midst of which sounded a great uproar and screaming in confusion. Something unusual must have happened.

"In Peter's little house—a terribly rich lady—an organ, four men couldn't carry it in, the door is too narrow—a little boy—before we came to school," the voices all sounded together so that Sally could understand nothing of what was being said. Then one voice called:

"All come with me! They surely haven't finished. Let us all go up on the Alm!"

And suddenly the whole flock scattered, and almost the entire crowd hurried up and away in the same direction. In the square only Heidi and Sally were left standing and looking at each other in surprise. Heidi had been describing with great vivacity something that had happened, but what it was or where it was taking place Sally couldn't begin to imagine.

"Please begin again at the very beginning and tell me everything, and where you saw it all first," pleaded Sally.

"Yes, indeed, but now listen," commanded Heidi. "You know very well that Peter lives with his mother and blind grandmother in a little house in a hollow halfway up the Alm. I brought them some presents when I came home from the Gemmi. Among them was a bolt of bright cloth which Brigitte made into curtains for the windows and covers for her furniture. Then she gave the living room and the bedroom next to it a terrible cleaning and said something about taking in someone to board. Then, just this morning when Peter and I were leaving for school, we saw a wagon and the horse could hardly pull it along, for there was an organ on it and other things, I believe, a little table and chair but really nothing more."

"But you said a very rich lady—"

"I think she is rich. Anyway," Heidi went on, "she

was very pale and she was wearing a silk dress, and
behind her was a boy, and nobody had seen them before.
Four men from the village carried the organ into the
house, but it wouldn't go through the door, and everybody standing there said she must be a terribly rich
woman to have such an organ. Nobody knows where she
came from and when they asked Brigitte, she only said,
"I haven't the time," and left everybody wondering that
such a rich lady should come to Peter's little board house.
Grandfather said long ago it would fall to pieces sometime. And you should see the woman, Sally. You would
wonder, too, why she had come there. Just think, on a
work day, she had on a black silk dress!"

"How did the boy look?" asked Sally, who had listened with great interest to the story.

"Well, only think, I had almost forgotten that," continued Heidi. "Think, he had velvet knickerbockers,
very short, black velvet knickers and a little velvet
jacket, just alike, and a little cap to match. Just think of
it, a boy with velvet knickers!"

"What does Peter say about it?" asked Sally.

"Nothing much. We just stood and stared at that big
organ, and then it was time for school."

"Heidi, do you know what? Come home with me, and
I will ask if I may go up to Peter's house with you. I
should like to see it, too," declared Sally.

Heidi was ready to carry out the proposed plan until,
quite suddenly, she remembered her violin lesson. The
new boy and the strange lady had put it entirely from
her mind.

The lesson went badly at first. Heidi was late and
when she started to apologize she forgot and said
"Teacher" instead of "Fräulein" as the young woman pre-
ferred to be called. Next she brought out a big singing
book and asked Heidi to read the notes. She was able to
read the words very well for she had often read them to
the blind grandmother, but the little black dots and the
lines confused her.

"Very well then," said the teacher. "I will play a little and see if you can follow. Come now, you did it before."

It took time, but at last Heidi was ready to try it again. They began with the easiest piece in the book. It was the tune to "Little Lambkins" but with different words:

> *"Little children, take care,*
> *Learn your lessons aright . . ."*

Heidi did not like it half as well as the lively song about the lambs, but the melody was the same and she was able to follow it. A second piece was undertaken, but they soon came back to the first piece and played it over and over until Heidi began to wish that Peter could be there beside her singing the words that had sounded so beautiful to their ears.

"Once more! Once more!" urged Fräulein Meili, and each time it went a little better.

"Soon I can play for the blind grandmother," Heidi started to say and then stopped for, all at once, it came to her that everything was changed at Peter's house and it might no longer be possible for her to go there. Then swift running was heard and in rushed Sally's two brothers.

"May we—to the Alm—people have come—a wagon and a big organ," both shouted together.

"No," exclaimed the aunt. "You have interrupted Heidi's music lesson."

"But she will tell you . . ."

So both began again and would have continued if Sally hadn't come in herself and made everything clear. Their mother was not pleased by the proposal that the children should run to Peter's house to see two strange people and add to the staring crowd, so they had come to the aunt hoping to obtain her permission. She would not allow them to carry out the plan, but as compensation, invited Heidi to have coffee with the pastor's children and afterwards play in the garden. Sally and Bruno were pleased and ran with Heidi into the house, but Max made a wry face, for wherever there was something remarkable to see and explore he wanted to be on hand. He stood silently and considered whether it would be of any use to interrupt his father in his study in order to obtain a final permission. But before he had come to a decision his aunt called:

"Well, Max, are you having coffee with us or not? Isn't there some old Roman or Egyptian who could not always do what pleased him? Just think about that and it may help you decide what to do."

This really was a help, for Max was an eager history student and immediately yielded to the suggestion and came in and seated himself with the others. Lisebeth served the coffee, muttering all the while she poured a little into Heidi's cup, then made it light with milk. This gave clever Sally an idea.

Afterwards, when they were playing hide-and-seek in the garden, she crawled in beside Heidi and whispered, "We'll ask Lisebeth to give us a little ground coffee to take to the blind grandmother tomorrow. She will surely permit it when she hears that her coffee mill is broken."

"What are you two whispering about?" asked Max, discovering their hiding place behind the hen house. "The game is over. Now come and tell us about it."

"We have a plan," Sally began.

"It is a way to see the new boy," Heidi put in eagerly.

"But you will see him anyway," said Max with a superior air. "He will naturally come to school."

"Naturally," affirmed Bruno, the little echo of his older brother.

The two girls were agreed that it would be better to wait, but the next morning when they arrived at the schoolhouse there was no strange face to be seen in the whole schoolroom, and everything went along in the usual way.

When school was out some ran one way and some another, but Heidi still stood there waiting for Sally. She would have liked to find out more about the strange boy and his mother from Peter before carrying out their plan, but Peter had not come to school. Then she saw Max dart like an arrow into a circle of boys, and all were making such extraordinary gestures and screaming together so unintelligibly that Heidi could guess more plans were being made, probably about the two strangers. She went slowly along and kept looking back, but Sally did not appear.

Finally she reached the church and then the parsonage. The pastor was just coming out of his study when the boys ran up to him, red-faced and panting.

"We have—something to settle—three verses."

"Sh! Sh!" said the father. "First think what you have to say and then say it. Speak calmly, one after the other."

There was a moment of subdued silence and then Max began eagerly:

"Think, Papa, we have made up a verse to sing to the boys who stay away from school. It goes like this:

"The Dörfli school is proud
  Of its gallant crowd
  And makes it hard for those who stay away.
  Any small dispute
  Will draw a new recruit
  And round up lazy boys who want to play."

"Isn't Max clever, Papa?" asked Bruno. "I helped him make up the last line."

"H'm," said the father, stroking his chin. "So now my boys are writing poetry."

"Do you think they will write a reply, Papa? If they do, we have another song to sing to them:

"If Velvet Knickers from the Alm
  Wants to keep it calm,
  Saying that he does not care to fight,
  We will treat him with despite—"

"But these are such fighting songs, Max," protested his father. "I much prefer that you stick to your history. Usually such poetry ends up with holes in your heads."

The boys, looking much disappointed, said good-bye to their friends and went inside. Heidi was inwardly furious. Peter was not lazy. She knew that. But why had he stayed away when she had so much to talk over with him, and where was Sally?

"And what have you been doing, Heidi? Why are you so thoughtful?" continued the pastor. "If you are looking for Sally you will find her in the kitchen with Lisebeth."

"Oh, then she has—" Heidi stopped herself as she was about to say, "gone for the coffee" and changed it to, "then she has already come home?"

"Yes, I believe she ran ahead of the others. Ah! Here she is now," exclaimed her father as Sally appeared with a small basket on her arm.

Lisebeth called after her from the kitchen door: "Tell Brigitte I send my regards. I have been wanting for a long time to make her a visit, but such as we are can't go away whenever we like. We have our work to do, but some fine Sunday I am surely coming."

"Aha, Lisebeth wants to see the strange people, too," remarked Max, poking his head out of an upstairs window.

Sally made a face at him, unobserved by her father, who might have detained her. "We are taking some coffee to the blind grandmother. We have permission. Come, Heidi," she said all in one breath.

"You may go, Sally," answered her father in reply to a questioning look from Heidi, "but I don't want you running into a house where you haven't anything to do, in order to see strange people. I trust you not to."

"No, Papa," Sally replied quickly. "We will bring the coffee and give Brigitte Lisebeth's message. Then we will come right home."

CHAPTER X

The New Arrivals

HEIDI WAS very happy. Soon she would see Peter and find out for herself the answers to all the questions that had been puzzling her. She stopped in at the manor house to tell the doctor where she was going, and gladly started off with her friend.

It was a bright, sunny day, and there was plenty of time. Sally took her hand, and the two of them started up the hill to the fir woods where the path ran for quite a distance in the shade. Here Heidi slackened her steps a little, it was so lovely in the shade of the fir trees where up in the branches the wind rustled so merrily, and all the birds were singing together. She felt like singing, too. Someday she would really make the violin sing like that. She could hardly wait to tell the grandmother she was learning to play it. Then her thoughts turned to the strange people, and she wondered what she would say to them if they came to the door when she knocked.

"Perhaps it would be better to just run in without knocking," she said to Sally when the two were climbing the sunny slope together. "I often do that when I come there alone."

"Do you run right to the grandmother?"

"First through the kitchen and then through the living room and then to the grandmother," Heidi explained.

"Her bedroom is back of the others and there are two more small bedrooms at the side."

Sally was surprised to hear that there were so many rooms in such a tiny house. It looked even smaller than it was as all but the roof and attic window were hidden in a hollow somewhat to the side of the path that continued up to the grandfather's hut far above. Heidi thought of him alone up there and her heart yearned towards him, but he would be coming down in another month when the days grew colder. He did come down on Sundays, and she always sat between him and the doctor in church.

"What are you planning, Heidi?" asked Sally, seeing her so thoughtful.

"Nothing. I was just thinking of the grandfather. I would be up there with him now if I didn't have to go to school."

"Not you, too?" exclaimed Sally.

"What do you mean?" asked Heidi, puzzled.

"Wanting to stay out of school. Max will really have something to sing about if you stay away."

"I don't like his song," declared Heidi. "Peter is not lazy. He works hard for his mother—chopping the wood, making the fire, and everything. Besides all that, he takes care of all the goats in the village and earns what little they have to live on."

"It is very little, isn't it?" Sally asked more sympathetically as they came closer to the small weather-beaten house and she could see for herself how poor it was.

The door was standing open to let more light and air into the dark kitchen. Beyond, in the living room, the children found themselves in sight of a dark lady sitting there sewing who, at their stormy entrance, raised her head and looked at them with large, sad eyes.

Sally grew scarlet and in her embarrassment stood as if nailed to the door, but Heidi ran on into the grandmother's bedroom and began telling her at once how she was learning to play the violin.

Meanwhile the lady held out her hand to Sally and said kindly, "Come in, dear child. What brings you here?"

Sally was completely bewildered. She no longer knew why she had come there, for she had not really come to bring coffee. She had only invented that excuse in order to come in where she had now arrived so unexpectedly. She approached the lady and tried to say something, but could not speak a word, but stood red and helpless as she had never done in her life before.

"Come, sit down beside me, dear child," the lady then said in such a gentle voice that it went straight to Sally's heart. "Come, let us get acquainted."

There was a sudden movement from one corner. Sally did not know what was there, for until now she had not dared look around her, but now she looked up.

A boy, somewhat taller than she, was bringing a chair and placing it very carefully in front of her. At the same time he looked at her with such a merry face and the restrained laughter showed so plainly in his eyes, that a complete change came over Sally and she burst out laughing. At this the boy, too, suddenly relieved his feelings with a ringing laugh, for the sudden entrance of the two girls and the confusion in Sally's face had amused him for some time, but he was too well brought up to break into laughter at once.

"Now, dear child, what brings you here?" asked the lady, smiling too, and speaking in a most winning tone.

"I have—I have—I wanted," began Sally hesitatingly. "I wanted to give a message to Brigitte and some coffee to the blind grandmother, and then I wanted—I wanted to see you." Sally could not stop at a half truth. The lady's sad, friendly eyes were directed towards her so penetratingly that she had to speak out everything exactly as it was.

"That is really very dear and friendly of you to want to see us, but how did you know we were here?" asked the lady. "Did your friend tell you?"

"Yes, she—she's Heidi," Sally began, still tripping over her words.

Then Heidi herself came in and told the boy and his mother how everything had happened, that she and Sally had wanted to come yesterday, but she had her violin lesson and today Peter was not in school so she could not ask him how the organ and all the lady's things would go into the little house.

Now, looking around, Heidi could see that there weren't so many things after all. She had expected to find the grandmother's chair and her spinning wheel gone from the window, but they were still there and there was really nothing different except the large organ and two or three more chairs and the bright curtains and chair covers dressing up the room.

Sally's eyes met Heidi's, and each understood what the other was thinking. The boy in his velvet clothes looked exactly like one of the knights in the big history book Peter had borrowed to read during the summer. Moreover, the lady in her black silk dress appeared so aristocratic and, at the same time, so sad, that they knew they should not have rushed into the house so unexpectedly. They remembered, too, that the pastor had said they must not go in especially to see these people, and that was exactly what they had done. Heidi rose hurriedly, for it had also come to her mind that she had not seen Peter and she really did want to ask him why he had stayed away from school.

"We must go now," she said quickly, holding out her hand to the lady, who took it and then shook hands with Sally, looking into her eyes so affectionately that Heidi knew she had really been pleased by their visit. She thanked them for coming and then she kissed each of them on the forehead and said, "You have brought a little laughter into this quiet house. Do come again."

"We will, thank you," Heidi promised as she pulled Sally along through the open door and out into the dark kitchen. The boy had rushed ahead of them to open the

outside door for them and was standing politely like a
doorman at the entrance to show them out.

"Thank you," Sally said, trying to be as polite as he
was.

"Aren't you coming to school with Peter?" Heidi
asked as they went out.

"No, my mother will teach me, but Peter is coming
tomorrow. He's outside somewhere helping his mother
find wood."

Heidi was glad to hear this. Now she could prove to
Sally and her brothers that Peter was not a lazy boy who
wanted to play as it said in their song.

"Well, good-bye," said Sally, holding out her hand to
the boy. "It was nice to meet you, but we still don't
know what your name is."

"Eric. And yours?"

"Sally."

"She's the pastor's daughter, and I'm Heidi. Are you
coming to Dörfli to church?"

Eric shook his head. "Father Klemens will instruct
me." Then he closed the door, leaving Heidi and Sally
almost as puzzled as they had been before they came.
Heidi was the first to speak.

"He was certainly polite."

"Too polite," agreed Sally. "I wonder what Peter
thinks of him."

They turned towards the path, still wondering. Before they reached it, Brigitte came towards them with a
big bundle of sticks on her head. Her appearance delighted Heidi. Letting go Sally's hand, she ran towards
her so violently that the poor woman started back with
her load and almost lost her balance.

"Mother Brigitte, you have such nice people in your
living room," Heidi exclaimed eagerly. "Do you talk
with them much? Where did you find them?"

"Now calm yourself; just be calm," said Peter's
mother, who had recovered her balance and was ready to
go on with her load. "I am all out of breath, but just tell

me how it is that you have gone in to see these people
with the pastor's daughter, and who knows how many
others you have sent? It is not like you, Heidi. The lady
is not well, and I try to keep the house quiet. They are
not people you can run into so freely; as if they lived
on the street."

"But the lady was so very friendly. She seemed to like
Sally especially," explained Heidi, for it suddenly came
to her mind that the pastor's daughter had forgotten to
leave her little basket of coffee for the grandmother, and
she had a message from Lisebeth besides.

"Really," Sally put in, "she was not at all offended,
just a little surprised, and the boy laughed."

"And well he should!" exclaimed the indignant Brigitte.

"We did not mean any harm," Heidi continued, trying to pacify her. "We just wanted to find out where
you were and why Peter did not come to school and
about the big organ. Does the lady play it? The grandmother would like to hear it if she does. I found her in
her bedroom and she said she was feeling poorly. She
might feel better if the lady played some of her
hymns."

"I'll speak to her about it," Brigitte promised. "You
understand, Heidi, that these people are paying me well.
The room is theirs now. If we come in there at all we
must come as their guests."

"But where do you stay?"

"Upstairs," Brigitte replied shortly. "If you come to
see us again you must come up the back stairway on the
outside of the house. Do you understand that, too,
Sally?" she asked, turning to Heidi's friend. "You won't
run in like that any more, will you?"

"No, I will not. I hadn't intended to do so again.
There! I have forgotten the most important thing.
Lisebeth sent ground coffee for the grandmother and
also sent her regards and she is coming to see you some
fine Sunday."

These last words sounded quite distant, for during this conversation Heidi had started to run and was already far away. After a few high jumps she reached the wooded place just beyond the house. Here Peter was standing with an axe in his hand, and Heidi could see he had been energetically chopping wood.

"I told Sally you were not lazy," Heidi called out to him, "but why didn't you come to school?"

"Well, is that you? Good afternoon! I didn't know who could be jumping along so, and I hadn't time to look," said Peter quite importantly. "You see why I didn't come to school. Besides, we will have fresh eggs now. I had to fix a shed for the new chickens. But come, I will show them to you."

But Heidi had only a little time left and Sally was waiting and would surely want to hear about something quite different from chickens, so she said decidedly:

"No, Peter. Maybe another time. I have seen the strange lady and the boy and just wanted to find out what you think of them."

"Him?" said Peter, shrugging his shoulders. "To be sure, I don't know what to think. I stay outside, and he stays inside with his mother. The eggs are for her."

"Well, I hope the grandmother gets one now and then. We brought her some ground coffee."

And before Peter could say thank you or recover from his surprise, Heidi was running downhill after Sally, who had already gone on ahead. Then she began to go more slowly for she and Heidi had so much to think out and talk over that they were quite unaware of the time and did not notice when they passed the manor house. On the low wall surrounding the parsonage Bruno was standing and beckoning to them.

"Come along a little faster," he called urgently. "Aunt has already looked at the clock twice. What did you find out? Did you see the goat boy?"

"His name is Peter," Heidi informed the impudent small boy, "and that is what he likes to be called."

"We saw the boy you and Max call Velvet Knickers, too," Sally put in, "and you could learn better manners from him. Are you coming in with me, Heidi?"

"Just for a minute. The doctor is expecting me home soon. Maybe he will know what is the matter with the lady. Brigitte said she wasn't well."

"Ask him, won't you?"

Heidi said she would, and the two of them entered the house with Bruno following behind. The pastor's family were grouped together in the living room. The mother and aunt were darning stockings, the father was reading a large church paper, and Max was reading too, his head leaning on both elbows, deeply absorbed in his history book. Sally burst in on them, dragging Heidi by the hand, and said in great excitement:

"Oh, Mother, you ought to have seen how friendly the lady was, and she is so beautiful and so gentle and so kind and quite a grand lady, and Eric is like a knight in his velvet clothes, and so polite. You ought to meet him, Max. You would surely become friends."

An uncomfortable pause followed this outbreak. Heidi looked at Sally in surprise. Had she entirely forgotten that they ought not to have burst into the house without knocking and that she had stated that the object of their trip was to take coffee to the blind grandmother? It must have come to her mind for she suddenly grew red.

"But my dear child," said her mother, "did you really, in spite of your father's warning against it, intrude on these strange people? How could you go into the house without any reason?"

"Not without a reason, Mamma," said Sally, still somewhat embarrassed.

"Lisebeth gave her some coffee for the blind grandmother and a message for Brigitte," Heidi explained as an excuse.

"Inquisitive Sally had to go to the kitchen to carry out her plan, that is clear," said her aunt, and she looked at Heidi as if she were disappointed in her, too.

Since the whole scheme now lay clear as day, both girls felt called upon to apologize. Relieved when their apology was accepted, they turned back with renewed eagerness to their story. There was still so much to describe, the big organ, the lady's silk dress and her sad face, and then again the knightly Eric with the happy laugh and the merry eyes. Between them, they painted a very vivid word picture.

"Brigitte says they pay her well and they really are very fine and the boy so polite," Heidi finished emphatically.

"Well," said Max, looking up from his book, "now Heidi has another friend. It will soon happen to him as it did to the princes in the Tower of London. They wore velvet clothes, too."

Leaving Heidi completely mystified, Max bent over his book again and read on, with no interest for anything else, not even Lisebeth's sudden call to supper.

CHAPTER XI

A Sunday Afternoon Visit

THE FOLLOWING morning Lisebeth stood waiting in the kitchen doorway when Heidi came by to call for Sally, making all manner of signs. Sally waved her schoolbag as a sign of understanding and called to Lisebeth as she ran past:

"When we come home from school. It is too late now!" and, followed by Max and Bruno, she and Heidi started off on the run.

Never had a teacher in Dörfli had such a time with the children as Fräulein Meili did on that day. It often happened that some would be restless and others more indifferent than usual, but there was always a number with whom she could work successfully. But today it seemed exactly as if a flock of enraged spirits had taken possession of the children. Peter was there, but he was not at all the friendly playmate Heidi had known ever since she first came to live with her grandfather. All the boys were casting furtive, warlike glances at each other, and muttered threats were hurled back and forth. When the teacher turned her back, such threatening gestures were made towards those facing her that they all rolled their eyes and were seized with such a desire to fight that friend or enemy made no difference.

Heidi and Sally, usually orderly and well behaved, put

their heads together and whispered as busily as brooks.
Heidi felt she had to know more about the princes in the
Tower of London, but Sally could tell her nothing
except that she had seen a picture in one of her picture
books of two frightened boys in velvet suits. "Underneath, it said, *The Babes in the Wood*," she finished in a
loud whisper.

"But that's a song. I started to read it to the grandmother once, but it was too sad," Heidi whispered
back.

Max, too, the best scholar, was off the track and stared
before him in deep thought as if he had not heard the
teacher's question.

"Max, I ask you once again. Will you tell me the
principal products of northern Italy?"

Italy! With this name the whole operation of war
came before his eyes, for Max had studied the regions
carefully where the Romans had met their enemies. Big
Churi had been chosen for the part of Hannibal, and
Max was considering how he could lead his troops
against him and show him how a great general goes to
work.

"Max," then said his aunt, as still no answer came,
"what there is in our subject so difficult of comprehen-
sion, I cannot see. But this I see, that all of you together
are like a flock of stupid sheep. Heidi, you magpie, can
you keep still a moment and listen when I speak?"

"I just wanted to ask—I mean, are the princes in the
Tower of London the same as the Babes in the
Wood?"

"Exactly the same," replied Fräulein Meili. "If you
will all be quiet and listen, I will read the story. The two
little princes, Edward and Richard, had a very tragic life.
Their father died when they were small, and his brother
was asked to help the Queen care for the boys since
Edward would someday be King. But the Queen dis-
trusted this uncle and hid the boys in a church. In

England at that time it was against the law to harm anyone who took refuge in a church."

Loud whispers interrupted her here, but soon the schoolroom became quiet again and she went on:

"They stayed there safely until it was time for Prince Edward to be crowned. Afterwards he was taken to the palace, but his uncle spirited him away and told him he would be safer in the Tower of London. His brother was thrown in the Tower, too, but not for long. Both were taken away in the night and at first the people thought the cruel uncle had left them to starve in the woods. A song was written to show their sorrow and displeasure."

Heidi raised her hand. "Could we hear it, please? Would you please play it on your violin?"

This request pleased Fräulein Meili. She took out the instrument, tuned it, and began the sad story. Heidi was in tears by the time she reached the end:

> *"And when they were dead*
> *The robins so red*
> *Brought strawberry leaves*
> *And over them spread.*
> *Poor Babes in the Wood!*
> *Poor Babes in the Wood!"*

"But it didn't happen that way!" cried Max, speaking out without first raising his hand.

"Well, if you are so eager to be heard, perhaps you can tell us how it did happen," his aunt retorted.

"Indeed I can. Two years later the castle steward and his helper confessed that they had been bribed to smother the princes in their sleep. They were buried—"

"That will do," then interrupted the teacher. "We have heard quite enough about the poor Babes in the Wood. Now we must come back to the present. Max, have you recovered from your daydreams enough to tell us the products of northern Italy?"

"The battles of northern Italy—"

"I said products."

"Oh!" Max looked so crestfallen that the whole
schoolroom rocked with laughter, all except Heidi, who
was still grieving over the fate of the princes in the
Tower of London and remembering that Max had said it
would happen exactly the same to Eric because of his
velvet knickers.

"We mustn't let it happen," she said emphatically to
Sally as soon as school was over.

"We mustn't let *what* happen?" her friend asked in a
puzzled way.

"We mustn't let Eric be smothered. Maybe Peter can
stop them. Peter!" called Heidi as he ran past her.

"Not now," he flung back at her in a great hurry.
"They are about to begin."

"I think they're choosing sides for some kind of war
game," reasoned Sally, "but don't worry, Heidi. Papa
will never permit it. Besides, Eric isn't coming to school
so they can't possibly hurt him."

Heidi was not so sure. Some unusual undertaking was
under consideration, for all the boys were crowded
together in a big throng, brandishing their uplifted arms
high in the air, and screaming with all their might.

When Sally noticed this well-known sign of a long-
drawn-out dispute, she seized Heidi's hand and pulled
her along toward the parsonage.

"You must come with me," she insisted. "Lisebeth
wants to hear everything that happened yesterday, and
you can tell it better than I can."

"Didn't she hear what you said at the table?"

"No," replied Sally. "She's old and her hearing isn't
very good except when you're up close."

"Well, then, we will tell her," agreed Heidi. "She and
Peter's mother used to be good friends. I'm going up
there again Sunday. The lady asked us to come again."

"I'm coming with you," announced Sally.

Heidi nodded encouragingly and they ran on, talking

over their plans, until they reached the parsonage. Lisebeth was there waiting for them. Interrupting each other and growing more and more excited the further they went, Sally and Heidi told her all about the knightly Eric and the dire prediction Max had made, comparing him to the princes in the Tower. But the liveliest of all was Sally's vivid description of the lady and her polite young son, their words and gestures and the way they were dressed and the superior manner they had. But suddenly, in the midst of this account, Lisebeth jumped up as if she had been stung by a wasp and said:

"What do you say, Sally? The lady is wearing a silk dress in the middle of the week? Silk? And goes and lives with a poor widow? And the boy wears velvet knickers and a velvet jacket, all of velvet? Well, well! I served your great-grandfather ten years, and your grandfather thirty years, and have lived twelve years with your father, and held him in my lap and seen him grow up from his earliest days, and both your brothers, and not one of them ever had any velvet knickers on their bodies, and yet they were all pastors, your great-grandfather, and your grandfather, and your father; and the two sons, one of them will be exactly the same, and yet none of them ever wore velvet knickers, and the lady in her silk dress, yes, indeed! There is something back of it, I tell you both, there is something back of it! But it must come out, and if Brigitte tries a hundred times to cover it up, I will bring it out. Velvet knickers, indeed! I only wonder what more!"

Sally and Heidi stood thoroughly astonished in front of the anger-flashing Lisebeth, and absolutely did not understand what had caused this outbreak, but they had had enough of it and turned and sprang away into the sunshine of a bright September day.

"What'll we do with the afternoon? Shall we go to your house?" asked Sally.

"Yes, I want to ask the doctor—"

But Lisebeth was not finished. She called angrily after

Sally. "Come back here! Come back here this instant!
There is going to be a thunderstorm; there is every sign
of it. You go on home, Heidi!" she added, "that is, if you
have a home. It seems to me the doctor allows you to run
about altogether too freely. There should be a woman in
the house to look after you."

Heidi wanted to say, "I look after myself very well,"
but, remembering Eric's polite replies to all her questions, she said instead, "Thank you for your interest in
me," and then ran on home to tell her godfather all that
had happened.

Meanwhile Sally was obliged to go inside although she
knew there was no thunderstorm brewing except in
Lisebeth's mind. Later she screamed at Max and Bruno
for coming in late and made supper so uncomfortable
that everyone was glad when it was over.

Afterwards the pastor went very quietly out into the
garden, for thunderstorms in the house were more dis-
tressing to him than any that might come from the heav-
ens. As soon as he left the dining room, Lisebeth planted
herself in the doorway, both arms akimbo and looking
very warlike, said:

"I think it wouldn't make any difference if I should go
to visit Brigitte. It is four years since I have been up to see
her."

This sounded very reproachful to the pastor's wife,
and she said soothingly:

"But Lisebeth, you surely couldn't think that a walk
to Brigitte's or wherever you liked, would be prevented.
We have allowed you to work for the doctor or whom-
ever you pleased and to go wherever you wished."

"Just as if there was nothing to be done in this house
and I only a visitor for fifty years and more!" was the
heated reply. "No, no, I know what has to be done, if no
one else knows. I can wait until Sunday afternoon. That
is a time when people like us can go out, and if it is
permitted by the pastor's wife I will go and not stay

away too long. Why, if an orphan child like Heidi no-
tices so much, surely there must be more."

"It is entirely all right with me," said the pastor's wife
again soothingly, "do just as you think best."

She added nothing more, for she had already noticed
that a fire of anger had been kindled in Lisebeth, which
would only blaze higher with every word that fell on it.
So Lisebeth muttered away for a while in the doorway
and then went back to the kitchen. But, until Sunday,
there was no more peace in the parsonage, and everyone
walked past Lisebeth as cautiously as if she were a
powder keg which, at any moment, might explode.

At last Sunday came. After dinner Lisebeth worked
around in the kitchen with a great clattering of dishes.
When everything looked clean and bright, she went to
her room and dressed in her Sunday clothes. Then she
said good-bye to everyone as if she were going on a long
journey, for it was an event to Lisebeth to go visiting.
She marched up the road, looking to the left and right to
see what was growing in this and that neighbor's field
and how the doctor managed in the big manor house
with no woman except herself to keep it clean and
tidy.

"I should be two people . . . three . . . four . . ."
As her inmost thoughts began to work again, she walked
faster and faster, talking to herself in an undertone as she
hurried on up the mountain. She was quite out of breath
when she arrived at Brigitte's little house.

From her window in the peak of the house Brigitte had
seen Lisebeth coming and was very much surprised that
this time she had kept her promise, as she had been saying
for several years that she was coming soon, and had never
come. Three days before, she had sent the same word
and here she was already.

Brigitte went to meet her old friend whom she had
known since childhood, and welcomed her in front of
the cottage. Then she led her guest around the house and

up the little wooden stairway behind. Lisebeth made her
way rather unwillingly. Even before she had climbed up
the stairs, she burst forth:

"Listen, Brigitte," she began, "when your mother had
her sight we used to come in through the kitchen and
then the living room and so upstairs. But now your oldest
friend has to come in at the back and up these rickety
stairs, and it surely must be on account of the strange
people you have taken into your house. I have heard
about them from Heidi and now see for myself what they
are compelling you to do, that you don't dare go through
your own living room."

"Heidi shouldn't talk so! It is not what you think!"
cried Brigitte, quite alarmed. "These people are not compelling me to do anything. They are so friendly and
gentle they even welcomed the children when they ran
in without knocking. Heidi is used to running about as
she pleases, but the pastor's daughter should have known
better. The lady does deserve privacy—"

"What about you and Peter?" Lisebeth interrupted.
"Wasn't this Peter's room up here? Where does he sleep
now, with the goats? And what about your poor blind
mother? The woman can do nothing to help her if she is
such a lady and wears a silk dress every day and her son
in velvet, no less! And why are they hiding so, in a little
cottage that really looks like a big henhouse. I will just
warn you, Brigitte, you will surely get into trouble with
such people."

"Lisebeth," said Brigitte more excitedly than she
usually spoke, "I have seen trouble before and will see it
again, but I could not, in good conscience, turn away a
sick woman."

"Sick woman, indeed! What about the boy?" then
questioned Lisebeth. "Is he sick, too, that he has to be
wrapped in velvet? There is something back of it that
will soon come out. Yes, indeed, wearing velvet knickers
and a velvet jacket besides, and such a vagabond nobody
knows where he comes from."

"Don't sin against the little boy," said Brigitte earnestly. "You would only have to look at him to know what an angel he is."

"Really," continued Lisebeth, "and when have you seen an angel, Brigitte, that you know exactly how they look?"

She would have gone on and on if, at that moment, the soft tones of an organ playing and the sound of children singing hadn't drifted up to her from below.

"Well," said Brigitte, "if you want to hear heavenly music, just stand there and listen. Have you ever heard anything sweeter?"

Lisebeth, for once, had nothing to say. A few moments later she followed Brigitte, down the inside stairway this time, and the two quietly entered the living room and seated themselves on the newly covered settee. The lady was at the organ playing for the blind grandmother, who sat in her usual place by the window, and the singers were Peter and Eric with Sally and Heidi joining in on the sad refrain:

"Poor Babes in the Wood!
Poor Babes in the Wood!"

CHAPTER XII

An Evening Hymn and What Followed

HEIDI FOUND herself in tears when the song was ended. The lady played so beautifully and the tones of the organ came out so deeply that the fate of the little princes grieved her more than ever and she could not stir from the spot where she stood between Eric and Peter. But Sally, seeing Lisebeth enter and seat herself beside Brigitte, turned to her and said:

"Oh, you are really here, Lisebeth. Papa said I could come if I would go home with you."

This pacified Lisebeth a little. She liked to feel the pastor's children depended on her. She turned to Brigitte and said in a more friendly tone:

"Come now to see me at the parsonage. It is a joy to behold such a beautifully ordered family and all together so fortunate and happy. You have the time now that there is somebody here with your mother. Does the lady play and sing for her often?"

"Every evening," replied Brigitte, "but this is the first time Peterli has joined in the singing. There is one song my mother prefers above all others."

"Yes, indeed," agreed the blind grandmother. "It always seems a great joy sounds through it. You know the song, Heidi. It is one you often read to me."

"Is it this one?" asked Heidi, opening the hymnbook

and forgetting, for the moment, that the grandmother could not see the words.

"Suppose I play it?" asked the lady.

"Sing it, too," begged Eric. "I feel so much better about everything when you sing. How does it begin?"

"Dear boy, it is a song about death," replied his mother. "Are you quite sure you want to hear it?"

Eric nodded solemnly.

"Oh, not that one," Heidi started to say. The song she often read to the grandmother was on the opposite page. But the lady was already singing so earnestly and so sadly that she could not interrupt:

> *"In pain I lay and languished,*
> *Death came to set me free;*
> *I stood in shame and anguished,*
> *Death gave me dignity,*
> *And raised me to high honor,*
> *And wealth beyond compare,*
> *Which cannot be diminished,*
> *As earthly treasures are!"*

While she was singing a great joy seemed to permeate the tones of the organ just as the grandmother had said. Eric was sitting on a low stool beside his mother, not singing this time, but looking up to her with his merry eyes as if he saw the vision, too.

"Such an organ belongs in church," was Lisebeth's only comment when the song was finished.

Heidi could no longer listen to the organ music and the lady's sad, sweet voice without weeping. As soon as she had thanked her and said good-bye to everyone else, she turned and ran after Sally, who was ready to leave with Lisebeth.

"Are you crying, too? I couldn't stand it any more," declared Sally, taking Heidi's hand.

Brigitte accompanied them a little way. She and Lisebeth were very talkative. Only when Lisebeth began to speak against the people she had taken in, Brig-

itte remained silent. They parted where the path turned
into the woods. Then Lisebeth strode on so energetically
that the children had to jump along very fast to keep up
with her.

That evening when Heidi lay down in her bed, although she felt very tired, she could not go to sleep; the
strange lady's song had made her so sad. She kept hearing
the solemn tones of the organ which sounded like weeping and rejoicing together. Would she ever be able to
play the violin like that? So far she had learned to play
only happy tunes. She tried to think of them to take her
mind off the lady's singing, but it was impossible.

Peter would tell her nothing. Why? Was there some
mystery about Eric and his mother that was being kept
from everybody? Lisebeth had said it would come out
and this worried Heidi. She heard the old clock in the
doctor's room strike eleven and then twelve, but still she
could not go to sleep. Then it seemed to her that she
heard a soft knocking downstairs. It was seldom that
anyone called the doctor in the middle of the night.
Perhaps he was sleeping. Heidi rose quickly and hurried
down to open the outside door.

"That's strange," she said aloud.

There was no one there. Then she noticed a faint
shimmer of light coming from the doctor's room, the
door of which was ajar. Heidi approached and was about
to open the door a little wider when she heard Peter's
voice:

"Yes, she is very ill. She was suffering so she had to
wake my mother, who told me to fetch a doctor and,
since you are the nearest—"

"Quite right, my boy," interrupted the doctor. "I will
go with you at once."

"It may be already too late," said Peter as they hurried
out.

They had not seen Heidi standing there in the shadow.
Now she was alone in the big house with only the dear
Lord to watch over her. Suddenly she realized she had

"It may already be too late," said Peter

forgotten her prayers. Kneeling beside her bed, she repeated every prayer she knew until finally, exhausted, she lay down on her bed and fell asleep.

"Heidi!" It was the doctor's voice calling her. "Hurry or you will be late to school. Lisebeth is here to fix your breakfast. We will both have dinner with the pastor's family tonight."

Heidi didn't ask why. She knew. All day, in school, she kept the knowledge to herself. Peter was not there and the other boys were occupied in taking sides for and against him. They had been forbidden by the pastor to sing the song Max had composed, and yet it sounded from every direction:

> *"The Dörfli school is proud*
> *Of its gallant crowd*
> *And makes it hard for those who stay away . . . "*

"Oh, Sally! They mustn't make it hard for Peter," cried Heidi, seizing her friend by the arm. "Can't you make your brothers stop?"

"Papa will stop them if I tell him—"

"Don't you dare tell!" cried Max, whirling around to face her. "You will spoil the whole battle plan. I am to be Fabius Tunctator and lead my troops up the hill where Hannibal can do nothing and not even give battle to me."

"Is Hannibal still alive?" asked Bruno, crowding close to his brother.

"Oh, Bruno, you are indescribably ignorant," remarked Max sympathetically. "He has been dead for more than a thousand years. But the leader of the stay-outers, Peter, is Hannibal."

"Not Churi? I thought you were going to fight big Churi and his army."

"No, you see, Churi is not a good Hannibal; he was a great and noble general. Peter is much better for the part."

"Max is right," declared Sally. "They're just playing,

Heidi. There's nothing for you to look so sad about. You're invited for dinner, you know, after your music lesson."

"But today is Monday," Heidi protested. "My lesson is on Wednesday."

"Aunt said it was today."

"Very well. I do want to play the violin. With just a little more practice I think I can play 'Little Lambkins' all the way through. It makes me remember that day when Peter and I went into the chapel—"

"And you saw the lambs. Oh, how I wish we had a lamb," Sally interrupted. "A gentle little lamb would make the boys forget their battles. Don't you think so, Heidi?"

"Maybe. The goats will be down from the pastures soon. Schwänli and Bärli are gentle."

"They're yours. I'd like a lamb for my very own."

Sally mentioned the lamb again at dinner table but the boys were talking over their battle plans so eagerly that no one paid any attention. Both boys became very dejected when their father reminded them that he had forbidden them to fight.

Heidi, usually such a lively guest, was not like herself at all. When the little golden baked apples came to the table Bruno stopped talking and applied himself industriously to eating. He emptied his plate in a very short time and looked questioningly at the others, for he knew the second serving would not come until all had finished the first. After watching Heidi for some time, he said seriously:

"Heidi, you keep swallowing as much as you can, but nothing can go down because you haven't put anything in your mouth and your plate stays full."

Then Heidi could bear it no longer. With difficulty until then, she had been swallowing down her tears and so kept very still. Now she burst into loud sobbing and brought out the whole story of how Peter had come for the doctor in the middle of the night.

"Poor Eric cannot eat today either," she finished, "for now his mother is dead. I heard Peter tell the doctor it was already too late."

Heidi wept still louder when she felt Sally's arms around her to comfort her. She could not control herself after she had held in so long. Bruno looked from one of them to the other, his puzzled face showing that he did not know whether he was to blame or not. Then the pastor's wife rose from the table, took Heidi by the hand, and led her into the next room.

The occurrence caused a great disturbance in the evening meal. The pastor was vexed and sat in silence. The aunt talked with increasing vivacity to emphasize this clear proof that children should go to sleep at once after they are put to bed. Max sat quite out of sorts before his plate, as if he had to eat sorrel instead of golden apples, for it made him very uncomfortable to think of death anywhere outside his history books.

When the doctor arrived, soon after, the pastor told him what Heidi had related in the midst of much sobbing, and the good man had to admit it was all true. Then the aunt asked the pastor if he did not think they ought to inquire who these people were, and perhaps do something for the boy, who was now apparently so alone. But the pastor was not of that opinion. He said these strangers had turned to Father Klemens, who was already there when the doctor arrived, so he could not interfere.

"There really must be relatives somewhere," the doctor agreed.

Possibly Father Klemens already knew much more about the people than anyone supposed. The lady would have been sure to turn to him, when she came to Brigitte's house as such a stranger and asked him to instruct the boy.

"But Papa, you must do something," protested Sally. "Heidi was so very upset."

"My dear child," replied her father. "You cannot follow Heidi in all her manifold impulses. She has too lively feelings and too little discernment to realize how these things must be done."

"I must now stand up for Heidi a little," said the doctor. "It is true that she has very lively feelings, but is this so undesirable? Where she finds sympathy and response she holds to her feelings and remains very warm and lastingly affectionate. How faithful she has been to all her friends! I would much rather have her go through life with her warm heart, believing she will find a friend in everybody, than to pass people by indifferently or direct hard criticism in their direction."

"There has been plenty of that," agreed the pastor. "Perhaps these tender-hearted children can lead us to some better way. Come, Sally, let us go now to Heidi and your mother. It has come to me that one more child in the parsonage might not be a bad idea. I'm sure Brigitte can hardly afford to look after Eric without pay. As for the organ, Lisebeth is right. It does belong in a church."

CHAPTER XIII

Further Events

WHEN IT BECAME generally known that the strange lady was dead, there was astonishingly much to talk about, especially by Lisebeth, who had seen for herself how everything was. Since not one of them really knew anything, each one of the village gossips had a different opinion. And when no relative appeared and the strange lady had to be buried without attendants, then a multitude of stories were circulated.

The bailiff of the community said she had evidently been an exile, and the justice of the peace added that she might have committed some crime. Lisebeth was not unwilling to bring such stories to the pastor and his wife, for she had been unable to get over her vexation about the velvet knickers.

Brigitte alone stood out against all the gossip and said to anyone who asked her that it was unjust and wicked to talk as they did for none of them had known the lady, or else they would have realized that there was nothing bad in her, but that she was an angel in kindness and tender-heartedness.

"She did say she had wronged someone, but she was near the end," Brigitte continued, "and I couldn't make out everything she was trying to tell me. It was something about a kind and affectionate father."

"Eric's father?" asked Peter, who could no longer contain his curiosity.

His mother shook her head. "I don't think so, Peterli. You remember that she told us the boy had no father on earth but that there was a Father in Heaven who would surely take care of him."

"It is not that simple," declared the overseers who had come to take account of what was left for Eric.

They found there was nothing at all except a few chairs, a single bed, and the organ which was promptly put in a wagon and hauled away. Eric had no clothes except the velvet suit which he wore. Then it had to be decided where he would live, for everyone took it for granted that he could no longer stay in the house where his mother had died.

"We can take care of him at the parsonage until we find out who he is and where he came from," the pastor offered.

The overseers were pleased with this proposal as much might be discovered if the boy would talk. So they went out together, satisfied. All this time Eric had been standing in a corner close to the blind grandmother, his big eyes fastened on the men. But he was very still, and when he wept he did so very softly, so that no sound was heard from him.

"Come," said the pastor's wife, taking him by the hand. "You are to stay with us in the parsonage."

"It is all right," Brigitte said, wiping her eyes on her apron. "You may come back to visit."

"So they are taking him away," murmured the blind grandmother as if speaking to herself. "The ways of the Lord are strange, indeed, that the old are left and the young taken."

"Be brave as your mother told you," Peter reminded Eric as he was led away.

The next day the pastor's wife decided it would be best for Eric to go to school and mingle with the children, so that he would be happy once more and a little noisy, for his soft weeping seemed to her much sadder than if he had made some sound.

She found suitable clothes and sent him off with Max and Bruno, but it was Sally who walked beside him. Eric went without protest. Whatever she told him, he obeyed at once. Thus it went on day after day, and Sally kept telling Heidi that Eric would gradually be as he was before, but the bright, sunny, merry face they had first seen was there no longer. A shyness had come into his nature, as if a safe, strong wall which had surrounded him and protected him had fallen away. The safe wall had been his mother's great love, and even the pastor could not make him understand that it was still with him.

In school Eric paid close attention to his books and seemed especially attentive when the teacher played the violin, but he never sang with the children and when the lessons were over he never waited until they collected in front of the school in order to make their way noisily home, but ran on ahead, either by himself or with Peter, and arrived at the parsonage alone. There he found his cup of milk and piece of bread on the table, ready for him, for Lisebeth refused to hand it to him. If the pastor's wife was there, she would say:

"Go out a little while with the children, Eric. It will do you good, and you can study your lessons afterwards."

Then Eric always went down and perched himself on the wall surrounding the parsonage garden. He remained there, watching the children running around and playing all sorts of games, but he never joined them.

He was watching in this way and looking in astonishment across the freshly mowed field where the whole crowd of school children were running and screaming, when Heidi saw him and ran directly towards him. The children were playing tag and big Churi was after her. As she knew what strong blows from his clumsy hands would fall on her back if she were caught, she rushed towards the wall, almost knocking Eric from his perch as she jumped behind it. In a moment Churi, hurrying after, would have caught her, but Eric darted forward, stretched both arms wide, and held Churi back. Then Heidi shot like an arrow around the parsonage garden, past the church and back again to the field, where having reached a safe goal, she could rest.

Churi growled: "Just let me go, or another time I—" whereupon he shook his fist at Eric, and ran off, for he hoped he could still catch Heidi.

When breathless Heidi had rested a little at the goal, she came running back, for she had recognized Eric's knightly help and was very grateful to him. She could not bear to see him always so alone, so she ran up to him and said encouragingly, "Come, play with us. You mustn't always go away by yourself. Can't we be friends?"

"No," replied Eric. "I can't play with you. I would not scream so terribly."

"You don't have to do that, it doesn't belong to the game. Just come!" and Heidi took Eric firmly by the hand and drew him along with her.

Eric then really played, and when he had once begun, he was very good at it. They had given up playing tag, and were in the midst of a ring game. The children had formed a large circle and were holding each other firmly by the hand. In the middle of the circle stood the leader. He had to hit someone's hand unawares and then start a race around the ring, to see who would win the open place first. The game was played with the greatest eagerness, but suddenly in the midst of it Eric broke away from both sides and ran off, so that a great disturbance followed.

"We won't have anything more to do with him!" exclaimed Churi angrily. "Who is he, anyway? And where does he come from?"

"It makes no difference. He can play with us anyway," declared Heidi stoutly. "If he comes back, he can come in beside me."

So it happened that the children went on with their play and Eric was forgotten.

The next day was Wednesday, the day of Heidi's music lesson. Eric was again sitting on the wall when she went inside the parsonage. But, as she was playing, she could see that he had come close to the window to listen.

"May I open the window?" she asked the teacher without telling her why.

"As you wish. Now shall we try 'Little Lambkins' once more, or is there some new song you would like to learn?"

"I think I would like to learn a hymn," replied Heidi. "If I had a violin I could play again for the grandmother as Eric's mother did. She played so beautifully, Fräulein. I wish you could have heard her."

"You will play beautifully some day yourself, my dear. Perhaps the organ would suit you better than the violin," the teacher suggested.

"I couldn't carry an organ around with me," replied Heidi. "I wrote and told my friend Klara I was learning, and she wrote back that a violin is best. It sounds like the wind in the fir trees when you play it, but I make it squeak like a mouse."

"It takes practice. Now once again:

> "Little lambkins, come down
> From the bright, sunny height . . ."

Outside a group of children had collected around Eric to listen.

"Whenever I hear that song I think I'll just die if I don't have a lamb of my own," declared Sally.

"Sh!" warned Kätheli, the innkeeper's daughter. "Eric will hear you."

"I did hear," Eric told them, "and you needn't think

you always have to whisper when I'm around. I don't
mean to spoil everything. You see, I am listening for a
song my mother used to sing, but it is not about lambs.
Right in the beginning it is about flowers and lovely
green trees, you know, with wonderful branches
and—"

"Just be still. I know it already," Sally interrupted
him. "Now I will sing it for you."

And with a steady voice and full tone Sally sang very
earnestly:

"*Three roses in the garden,*
Three fir trees in the wood.
In Summer it is lovely,
In Winter it is good.

"Is that it?" she then asked, full of confidence. But
Eric shook his head very decidedly and said:

"No, no, that is not it. What you sang is not in the least
like my mother's song."

All the children were very much surprised. "But there
are flowers and trees in it," one said, and another added,
"Do you really know yourself how the song begins,
Eric?"

"Yes, yes indeed," he answered. "You see, at first there
is a great festival, where they all come with many flowers
and green garlands, and they throw them because a great
gentleman is coming and—"

"Perhaps a count," interrupted Kätheli. "Was your
father a count, Eric? Did you live in a castle?"

"No," replied the boy seriously, "but my mother
did."

"Velvet Knickers used to live in a castle!" sounded a
mocking chant from behind them.

Churi and some of his soldiers were there ready to
make war on Eric, but the pastor came out and chased
them away, calling Max and Bruno inside. When Eric
and Sally were by themselves, Sally said:

"Now I surely know your song, Eric. If you had

spoken about the count at first I would have known it at once. Now pay attention!"

And she sang again in full tones:

> *"I stood on a lofty mountain,*
> *And gazed into the vale;*
> *I saw a shallop floating,*
> *Wherein three counts did sail.*

"Now, is that it, Eric?"

But Eric shook his head harder and said sadly:

"Not at all! Not at all! Perhaps the song is lost and nobody knows it any more!"

"Now I know another way," said kind-hearted Sally, for Eric's grief went to her heart. Whereupon she called loudly through the window, "Heidi, is your lesson almost over?"

"It is quite over," snapped her aunt, "now that you have interrupted it."

Moments later Heidi came bounding outside to see what Sally wanted. Breathlessly, Sally explained it. She fully expected that Heidi, who had read so many hymns to the blind grandmother, would know this one at once. But Heidi was more interested in what Eric had to tell her about the castle where his mother used to live.

"Was it old and gloomy or full of treasures like the big castle in Liechtenstein?" she asked eagerly. "Another few hours of climbing and we would have reached it that day Peter and I met those children from Nolla."

"What children?" asked Eric. "I have told you nothing. What do you know about Nolla?"

"The little boy said they came from there, that's all," Heidi replied, somewhat puzzled. "They are the grandchildren of Willow Joseph, the basketmaker, and I would like to see them again. We met them near the chapel the day all those playful little lambs were being driven down the slope. I became so excited just thinking about it that I played badly and Fräulein closed the window."

"That was because of Churi's screaming," declared Sally. "Papa is very angry at the boys for wanting to join the army against him. He will be angry at me, too, if I don't go inside. I thought you would know Eric's song right away, Heidi. Could you look through the grandmother's hymnbook the next time you visit her? I will hunt for it in my own singing books this evening. We have to find it or else Eric will be sad again."

Heidi agreed they must not let that happen. Then she shot away to tell her grandfather and the doctor all about it, and Sally went thoughtfully into the house.

It was late and there was already a light in the living room where the mother and aunt were sitting at the table, and even the father had settled himself. The boys, under his watchful eye, were studying more industriously than usual. Then Sally came in carrying four or five books of different sizes under each arm. Out of breath, she put down her uncomfortable burden.

"Oh, of all things in the world!" exclaimed her aunt in dismay. "Now Sally is going to be a history searcher like her brothers."

"No, indeed," opposed Sally, "but just give us a little room. I have to hunt for something with Eric."

The boys, busy with their own books, moved over, but Sally did not remain undisturbed for long. Soon they became interested in what she was doing and crowded towards her again while Eric retreated to his usual chair in the corner.

"There is nothing to be afraid of," Max told him. "I was just going to ask Sally why she had chosen a book of war songs to study."

"War songs!" exclaimed Sally, dropping them as if they had been nettles.

"Aha!" said Bruno, and chuckled a little. "Eric is now ready for battle. Why doesn't he let Max make up his song?"

CHAPTER XIV

The Battle Plan

JUST AT this time the collected inhabitants of Dörfli and the surrounding villages were in great suspense and anticipation over a matter which gave them so much to talk about that they could hardly carry on their daily tasks. Lisebeth had started a rumor that the lady's organ was to be given to the Dörfli church in payment for Eric's board at the parsonage and now it was an established fact. The new organ was to be dedicated the following Sunday.

The approaching festival gave the school children occasion for much loud talking. They had formed two parties, the churchly and the unchurchly, for some wanted to go to church Organ Sunday, as they designated the festival for short, and hear the organ played. But a great many of the others would have nothing to do with it.

Peter especially was against the morning service and, to Heidi's great disappointment, joined big Churi and his army of the unchurchly. There was to be a great battle and Churi had determined that it should be held on Organ Sunday. Peter and some of the others thought some other time would be more suitable than on a festival day. But Churi became quite wild when anyone said a word against his plan, and no one dared make him cross as he had so many soldiers under him, and only with his help could the victory be won.

Max was elected the leader of those who would go to church on Organ Sunday. He did not like to oppose peaceful Peter, but a battle against Churi and some of his followers suited him exactly. It seemed much more exciting to him than sitting around after the festival with the women and their baskets of food and listening to more unkind things being said about Eric and his mother. He did not mind that his army was small as there rose before him all the shining examples of the small Grecian army against the immeasurable Persian hosts, but he dared not say a word about his plans for he knew his father's aversion to such warfare, and particularly on Organ Sunday.

Churi had ordered his troops to assemble on the Friday before Organ Sunday, in the field, so that he could arrange for everything. So the whole army came together right after school and an indescribable uproar ensued. But big Churi could shout above them all, and explained the order for the day. First, all would assemble near the church, and during the service he would go with his officers to find out where the best place would be for their camp and the battle.

"So that's it!" exclaimed Peter, not so slow this time to understand what was in Churi's mind. "So you are planning to wait until everyone is inside the church so that you and your officers can do whatever you like on the outside."

"It has to be so on account of the arrangements," Churi called back angrily. "If you don't like it, drop it, and join the churchly crowd who have helped themselves to the organ that should have been left in your own house or sold to pay for Eric's keep."

Peter could not do that, in good conscience, and so everything went as Churi desired. After the dedication of the organ in the morning, as soon as it was mealtime, the whole army was to assemble immediately, and in the

morning only Churi with his officers should take off to
arrange all the positions. This was what Churi wanted.
The officers, chosen by himself, were all his good friends.
Peter was not one of them. As he listened to the battle
plan he became more and more suspicious.

The year before, just as September was ending, these
same boys had broken into the justice's vineyard and had
carried off all his beautiful Alsatian grapes. Peter suspected Churi planned to do the same thing again with
his trusted companions, and he wanted no part of it.

"I resign," he said suddenly. "My goats are all the
army I want."

"That is impossible!" screamed Churi. "You already
know the battle plan. You will betray us before the
enemy."

"I want nothing to do with it," replied Peter as he left
the field.

"Deserter!" screamed Churi.

Peter walked on, paying no attention. But now Churi
became fearful. This year the justice might be on guard.
He knew that in the afternoon the justice's wife usually
went out to walk in the vineyard, and in the evening
they both often went together, so that during church
service would be the only safe time for the boys to go
there. The justice and his wife were sure to be in church
on Organ Sunday so there would be no one to identify
the culprits.

As soon as the plans were complete, the crowd of boys
scattered in every direction. Now a crowd of girls gathered in the field, Heidi among them. She had not seen
Peter walk away or heard the call of "Deserter!" and so
she supposed he was still a soldier in Churi's army. Sally
was there, too, as she was always first on the spot whenever there was anything to see or hear.

"Max says I may recruit soldiers for him," she told
Heidi, "but everyone has taken sides except Eric. There
he is now!"

Eric was standing by a tall hedge. He had been there a

long time, watching the screaming throng from a distance. Sally ran up to him.

"This will be the biggest battle ever," she called out. "Wouldn't you like to be in it, Eric?"

"No," he replied decidedly.

"Why not?"

"Because I don't like what they are doing."

"But it is only a make-believe army, and Max needs more soldiers," Sally insisted. "Wouldn't you like to help him?"

"No."

"You'd better help," spoke up Kätheli, the innkeeper's daughter. "Even Peter, the goat general, is helping, and you'd better join the army, too, unless you want to go to the auction."

"What's the auction?" asked Eric, listening more attentively to Kätheli.

"There are a great many people in a room and they bid for you, and whoever bids the least wins you."

"That is stupid," said Eric.

Heidi thought so, too, but Kätheli went on describing what she had heard people saying at the inn. It was true that orphan children were sometimes awarded to the townspeople in this way. It had nearly happened to Heidi herself when the grandfather refused to send her to school. Now he enjoyed seeing her run off with the other children.

"Now do you think it's stupid?" asked Kätheli when she had finished describing everything in detail.

"Yes," replied Eric, "because they would get more money if they gave me to the one who bids the most."

"Oh, you don't understand it at all! You are not sold, just the opposite," explained Sally. "The one who wins you gets money or some possession of yours, like the organ. But that has already been awarded to the church because you are living at the parsonage with us."

"I would rather live on the Alm with Peter and his mother and grandmother. It is not so noisy there," said

Eric. "Nobody asked me where I wanted to live when they took the organ away."

"Can you play it, Eric?" asked Heidi.

He shook his head.

"But you could learn. Maybe Fräulein would teach you. I think she's going to play it in church. I can hardly wait to hear it."

"But Heidi, it isn't fair," Kätheli objected. "Now they've got the organ, Eric will be awarded to another home. That's what everybody was saying at the inn. The justice was there and he said so, too."

"Why?" demanded Eric.

"Well, you see, there is a chest with money in it for poor people, those in want and the homeless."

Eric grew very red at these words from Kätheli.

"I will not go to the auction," he said defiantly.

"Well, Eric, you have to obey the justice of the peace. If you don't obey him, someone takes you by the arm and carries you to the auction."

Saying this, Kätheli turned and ran off with Sally, who had decided to find out the truth of the matter from her father, while Heidi tried to comfort Eric.

"I don't believe you have to go to any auction. The pastor would not allow it. He is really very kind. You have a good home at the parsonage as long as you want it. Really, Eric," Heidi finished, "there wasn't room for the organ in Brigitte's little house."

"Or room for me, either? I don't want a home if I have to pay for it with my mother's organ! I can work."

An expression of defiance and anger flashed from Eric's blue eyes as he spoke. Heidi had never seen him like this before. He was still standing there, looking angry when Churi came past on his way home.

"Has somebody made you cross, Velvet Knickers?" he asked in a sneering tone.

Eric made no answer.

"Just come with us into the fight, and strike out, that will make you feel easier," Heidi heard him say. She had darted behind the hedge when she saw Churi coming and now it seemed safer to remain there.

Eric shook his head.

"Don't be so dumb and tell me something. The boy that made you cross will be sure to be on the spot, and you can just go for him."

"It is no boy," growled Eric.

"Well, what then? Could it have been Heidi? I saw you talking with her a minute ago. Where did she disappear to? Do you know?"

Again Eric shook his head. "No, it was not Heidi. It was Kätheli, the innkeeper's daughter, and I will not go to the auction," Eric burst forth, and his eyes flashed as never before.

"So it is only that. That's nothing but talk," said Churi. "Just come with us, and you'll forget the auction at once. Or are you afraid of a thrashing, you fine Velvet Knickers? Do you know what? I have a task which will surely please you."

A thought had just occurred to Churi. The justice's vineyard might not be safe, even on Organ Sunday. None of his friends wanted to go there, and he himself would rather let some other boy try and see if any trap had been laid, into which the first one would fall, while the others would be warned. Eric suited him admirably for this post.

"Now what do you say?" he urged silent Eric.

But Eric shook his head in refusal.

"If I help you, so that you will not have to go to the auction, will you then?"

"How can you do that?" asked Eric doubtfully.

"If I want to, I can," boasted Churi. "I'll speak to Father Klemens about it. He goes into all the houses along the whole mountain, far down beyond Maienfeld, and knows all the people and can provide whatever he likes for you. You only have to say what you want to do; tend cows or sheep and take care of motherless lambs, carry letters or whatever you would like best."

Eric had never heard any lying, so he believed every word that boastful Churi told him. He considered it for a moment and then said:

"What must I do for it?"

"Something that you will find the jolliest thing you have ever done. You can go out with me and the officers in the morning. You will be the spy and always go ahead, to find out if the land is safe, and where the best place will be for our camp and to give battle. But I tell you, you must obey me. I am the commander-in-chief, and if you do not do on the dot what I tell you, it will be the worse for you. First we are going through a vine-yard—"

"You can't have a fight there or even camp."

"That is no matter," continued Churi. "Listen to what I tell you. You must go through there and not make any noise, do you hear? And not run away, or—"

Churi raised his fist threateningly in the air.

"You mustn't tell anybody beforehand where we are going, do you hear?"

"I will not come with you," said Eric.

"Then go to the auction, that is the best thing for you. Now I am going, sleep well!"

But Churi remained standing, nevertheless. The blood rose once more in Eric's cheeks. He hesitated for a moment and then asked:

"Can I surely go where I shall have work to do? I should like to tend lambs or carry letters."

"Surely you can," muttered Churi.

"Then I will go with you."

"Then shake hands."

Churi held out his hand and Eric took it. Churi held his hand fast.

"On Sunday at seven o'clock, be there under the apple tree on the field. Say: 'I promise!'"

"I promise," said Eric in a very loud voice.

Churi let go his hand and they walked away from the hedge together. Heidi had not heard where or when they were planning to meet, but what she had heard was enough to almost break her heart. She believed that Peter, as well as Eric, had fallen under the influence of Churi and his mates, and she could think of no way to stop them from taking part in the big battle that would begin right after church.

CHAPTER XV

What Happened on Organ Sunday

EARLY IN THE morning, about nine o'clock, long before the time for church service to begin, large flocks of people were wending their way towards Dörfli, for everybody wanted to hear the new organ, and it was a glorious Sunday when everyone was all the more glad to go to church.

The women all carried flowers in their singing books, and when they reached the open space in front of the church, stopped and greeted each other, and stood around in groups engaged in conversation. Little by little the men, too, came along and did the same.

The doctor was standing a little distance away talking with the justice of the peace. Heidi let go her grandfather's hand and came closer to listen to the conversation, in which much appeared to be menacing, for the justice frequently raised his forefinger and shook it back and forth in the air.

Then the bell began to ring, and immediately the pastor's wife and Sally came out of their house, behind them Max and Bruno, very serious with their singing books under their arms. The battle had been forbidden, but they did not look as if the prospect of a peaceful Sunday morning pleased them very much. After a few steps, they all stood still, evidently to wait for the pastor.

Heidi was quick to take advantage of this pause. She shot like an arrow away from her godfather and grandfather and drew Sally quickly to one side.

"Just think what I know now, Sally," she whispered excitedly into her ear. "Yesterday evening Peter told me it wasn't at all on account of the battle that Churi's officers wanted to start off early in the morning, but that he thinks they are going into the justice's vineyard and take his Alsatian grapes, and Churi has persuaded Eric to go, too. He will be sent ahead, through the vineyard, for there might be some trap laid; then naturally Eric would fall into it, and the others could slip out at the side and nothing would be done to them. Now the justice has just told the doctor that he does have a trap into which anyone may fall and be smothered just like the princes in the Tower. What will we do, Sally? How can we stop Eric from going?"

"Oh, Heidi! It is much too late," answered Sally. "They went off early in the morning. Eric slipped out of the house without anyone seeing him. He must be already trapped."

Eric had kept his appointment in spite of the pastor's stern order that there must be no Sunday battle. He was on the spot long before Churi and his followers arrived. Although the boys started on their way to the vineyard as soon as they were all assembled under the apple tree, they met scattered churchgoers on their way. There were many people who wanted to see how everything looked in the fields, and so they had started early.

Churi had ordered each of his officers to bring a basket with him, for there would be no time to eat the grapes beforehand, but they must cut them off quickly and throw them into the baskets; then they would betake themselves to a safe place in the woods, and eat them there in peace.

Armed with baskets, the officers looked a little suspicious. Churi felt this, and ordered his companions to hide with him behind a barn until all the churchgoers should be inside, and then the way would be safe. Twice already, Eric had asked why they needed baskets on a march to battle, but he had received no answer.

As the warriors sat hidden behind the haystacks and there was more time for questions and answers, Eric asked again, "What are you going to put in these baskets?"

"Grapes, if you must know!" declared Churi, "and you will find them very good, once we have captured them."

After the bells had stopped ringing and everything had become still all about, Churi gave the order to start.

"But go past the church softly, do you hear?" he commanded, "for the doors are still standing open."

Full, clear organ tones sounded through the open doors as the boys drew near the church and then, with one accord, the whole congregation began to sing in a loud chorus:

> "How can I best receive Thee,
> How come before Thy face,
> Thou whom the whole world longs for,
> My soul's eternal grace!"

Like lightning Eric shot out of the midst of his companions away to the door and into the church. Churi became white with terror. He thought nothing else but that Eric had darted in there to betray them before the whole congregation, and to openly announce the proposed theft of the grapes.

Immediately he turned and ran with what he believed must be half the congregation at his heels. He could hear whole crowds coming along behind him, but they were his comrades running after him in the greatest haste, for when they saw bold Churi fleeing in such a manner, they thought the danger must be great, and chased behind him in more and more furious leaps.

Eric had run into the midst of a crowd of people all standing in the aisle of the church, because there was no

room left in the seats, the church was so full. Then the
singing with the organ accompaniment like a lofty tor-
rent rose through the church:

> *"Thy Zion is embowered in palms,*
> *And dark green branches bend,*
> *But I will cheer my soul with psalms,*
> *And to their words attend.*
> *My heart for Thee shall service claim,*
> *In constant prayer and praise,*
> *And I shall do Thy holy will,*
> *Through all my nights and days."*

Eric stood breathless as he listened, for it was his
mother's song. Fräulein was playing it exactly as *she* used
to play it for the blind grandmother. What joy it had
brought her, at the last, to know her music was so appre-
ciated. Now the same organ pealed out the same song for
the entire church. Eric knew it was right that his
mother's song should live, and yet the thought of someone else taking her place at the organ made him tremble
in every limb while great tears ran down his cheeks.

Heidi had not seen him run into the church. When
Sally went in with her family, Heidi knew that she must
go in, too, but she could hardly walk, from fear and
sadness. Now, as she sat in her seat between the doctor
and her grandfather, she saw and heard nothing at all of
the organ festival, for she kept thinking how Eric must
be trapped under sticks and leaves in a dark hole out in
the justice's vineyard, and her tears came so copiously
that she could no longer look up. But the Alm Uncle, as
the villagers still called her grandfather, noticed the
trembling boy and made a little room for him so that he
could sit down.

The song had stopped, and the pastor began to preach.
During the sermon Eric recovered from the strong feelings which had overpowered him when he suddenly
heard his lost song resounding in such mighty tones.
Then he looked around him and saw Heidi. Her eyes

were red as if she had been crying, too. He wanted to comfort her, but dared not reach across the fierce old man between them to touch her hand. Then their eyes met and smiles broke through the tears.

"Oh, Eric, you are not smothered!" Heidi exclaimed, beside herself with joy.

"No, certainly not," whispered Eric, surprised that Heidi should forget herself and speak out loud in church. Several people turned their heads and the grandfather said, "Shush!" in a voice that made him seem more awesome than ever to frightened Eric, who sat as still as a mouse until the whole sermon and the prayer had come to an end. Then the clear tones of the organ pealed forth once more, and again the congregation joined in and sang:

> *"Oh, God of Love, oh, Father-heart,*
> *In whom my trust is founded,*
> *I know full well how good Thou art,*
> *Even when by grief I'm wounded."*

When the song was over the Alm Uncle placed his hand on Eric's shoulder and said kindly, "Remember that, my boy, whenever you are in trouble. Why were you weeping so hard at first?"

Eric swallowed hard, but was unable to answer.

"This is my grandfather," Heidi explained. "You don't have to be afraid of him."

"I'm—not afraid," said Eric, still trembling.

"Then why were you crying? Was that the hymn your mother sang at the last?"

Eric nodded, but still he could not speak.

Heidi would have questioned him further. She would have liked to ask him at once how everything had happened, but when she saw how frightened he was, she hesitated, and only held him silently by the hand as they walked out of church together.

When they were outside and the crowds had thinned a little, the pastor came up to Eric and said in a fatherly

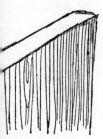

way, "Come with me to my study. We have something
to discuss."

Eric went willingly. As soon as they entered the study,
the pastor showed him a chair and said, "Now sit down
here in front of me and look me in the eyes and tell me
everything from the beginning, why you left the house
so early and what you intended to do."

Eric looked with his clear, blue eyes very straight at
the pastor and told him everything; how Kätheli had
said he would have to go to the auction, what Churi
had promised him, and how then he had taken part, and
still further, how all the others had brought large baskets with them, but he had none for he did not know
until then that they planned to steal grapes.

The pastor nodded his head in understanding. Sally
had already told him how Heidi had heard that the
justice was waiting with a trap to catch the grape thieves,
and it was now quite clear that in former years the gang
of boys, under Churi's leadership, had plundered the
vineyard.

"Eric," then said the pastor earnestly, "was it your
conscience that sent you running away from your companions into the church?"

"No," replied Eric. "It was because I heard my
mother's song."

"I see. Can you understand now that she is still guiding
you with her love? Joining a company of boys who rove
about on Sunday, while the bells are ringing for church,
and having to hide from good people behind a barn is not
something you learned from your mother, is it, Eric?"

Eric had to cast down his eyes as he answered softly,
"No, sir!"

"But there is something still worse, when one goes
with bad boys," continued the pastor. "He often gets
where he never wanted to be. You see, if you had not
been saved through your mother's song, you would have
been caught as a thief in the vineyard and severely pun-

ished. Eric, suppose your mother had to hear that!"

Eric grew very red. For some time he was silent, in evident distress and perplexity, then he asked abruptly, "Now can't I ever be a man of honor?"

"Surely, Eric," said the pastor. "That is what your mother wanted you to be, isn't it? If you remember the last verse of her song—

> *'And I shall do Thy holy will*
> *Through all my nights and days'*

then you will become a real man of honor. Will you think about this, Eric?"

"Yes, I will," Eric gladly promised and then looked up once more freely and openly at the pastor.

"And now," said the pastor, after a while, "something more, Eric. Are you content to live at the parsonage?"

Eric shook his head. "It is not on account of the organ. I want the church to have it. There was no one to play it any more at Peter's house, but it is peaceful there. Max and Bruno are always making up songs and planning some great battle. I would rather live where there is something more to do."

"Like carrying letters or taking care of motherless lambs?"

"Yes, Churi said I could do that. Then I could pay for my keep and not have to go to the auction."

"But that is only for the homeless. Don't you have any relatives at all?"

"I don't know," said Eric, quite distressed.

But the pastor said, in a very friendly way, "We will try and find someone. Is Eric Wall your full name?"

"It is Wallerstätten, after the castle, but that is like my velvet clothes, something for the boys to laugh at. I am no longer Henrico Wallerstätten, but the orphan, Eric Wall. Must I go right away to the auction?"

"No, no," replied the pastor quickly. "You are not going there."

Outside the door Bruno had his ear pressed close to the keyhole, listening, but he could hear nothing of the angry tongue lashing he had expected.

"Now Eric will catch it," he had said to Max when he saw his father leading him into the study.

Sally, too, feared Eric was in for a sound scolding.

"He's lucky," Max said, "you could count the black and blue spots on him if he had begun in front of the church and served under Churi."

This was enough to make Sally break forth: "You would be leading an army yourself if Papa hadn't forbidden it."

Max grew very red, for he recalled how long he had searched for some example from history so that he could justify the Sunday battle before his father.

"Listen to this!" Bruno called now from the door. "Eric says he was named after a castle and that his full name is Henrico Wallerstätten."

"Henrico!" exclaimed Sally. "Wasn't that the name of the Alm Uncle's brother? I must run at once and tell Heidi."

"Tell her Eric knew what he was doing when he ran into the church," Max called after her. "A church is supposed to be a safe retreat when the enemy gets too close—"

"What's this about the enemy?" asked the pastor, suddenly opening the door. "I have heard enough of such talk. If you had a gentle little lamb of your very own, do you think you could forget about fighting and take care of it?"

"Oh, yes, Papa!" cried Bruno. "I would be as peaceful as the lamb. Wouldn't you, Max?"

"A lamb would be a fine present," the older boy agreed. "Would it belong to all three of us?"

"All four of you," the pastor corrected him. "You're forgetting Eric. What do you think of the idea, Sally?"

But Sally was already hurrying away to tell Heidi Eric's true name was Henrico Wallerstätten and that, because of him, their father had promised to give them a lamb to keep the peace.

CHAPTER XVI

A Name for the Lamb

FROM THAT day on, no breakfast, dinner or supper passed in the parsonage that the children did not break forth, one after another, with these words:

"When are we going to get the lamb?"

Finally the pastor had heard enough of it. He had met with the justice of the peace and told him how Eric had spoiled the grape-thieves' sport and had caused Churi to run away before he noticed no pursuers were at his heels, but only his own gang chasing behind him. The justice was both pleased and amused at the way the affair had turned out and, since he considered Eric as the savior of his vineyard, he had come to talk over some reward when the question came again: "When are we going to get the lamb?"

The very next day, when Heidi had finished her music lesson, she was invited into the living room to play for the pastor's children. Eric was there, too, now very much at home in the parsonage and Peter had stopped by for a visit with him. The pastor encouraged this friendship since Peter was the only one, of all the boys in the Dörfli school, who had refused to take sides in the battle that had been planned for Organ Sunday.

So it happened that there was quite a chorus to sing

along with Heidi as she played the violin. They were all singing at the top of their voices:

"Little lambkins, come down
From the bright, sunny height—"

when suddenly the pastor opened the door and in sprang a real, live lamb.

Heidi was so surprised that she nearly dropped the teacher's violin, but Peter had a wide grin on his face as if he already knew what was about to happen. The lamb was covered with curly, snow-white wool and was as lively as any they had seen in the flock on the hill above the lonely chapel.

"Oh, Peter, did you—" Heidi began. But such a noise was raised in the room that not a word could be understood, for the lamb ran bunting and bleating from Max to Sally and back again to Heidi. Eric hugged it once and then little Bruno ran after it, screaming with delight. But suddenly sounded the pastor's commanding voice:

"Now, that is enough! A lamb does not belong in the living room. Peter will take its collar and lead it to its brand-new stall and the rest of you may come along and learn how to take care of it."

Heidi followed Peter and the lamb with Eric and Sally and her two brothers close behind her. The pastor went ahead until he came to the stable where he kept his fine team of horses.

"Won't the horses hurt it with their big hoofs?" asked Sally.

But Heidi, running ahead, had discovered a partition of brand-new boards that had been put up in the back of the stable. In it lay fine, soft straw for the lamb to sleep on. A little crib had also been brought in, where the children could throw grass and hay and other good things for the little creature to eat.

"May I feed it?"

"May I?"

"May I?"

All the voices sounded together.

"Later," said the pastor. "The lamb is not hungry now. It is time for it to rest."

When the lamb had been put to bed on the straw, and lay quite still, only breathing a little anxiously, the pastor said it must be left alone until it became used to its new stall. He showed Eric how to close the low door and told him the justice had given the lamb into his special care because he had saved the vineyard.

"But isn't it ours, too?" asked Max, looking a little disappointed.

"Certainly it is yours, too," replied the pastor, "but only as long as you are willing to take care of it. This helpless little lamb has been taken away from its mother and brought to you. Now you must take the mother's place, watch over it carefully and tend it so that it will be content with you and not die of homesickness."

"We mustn't let that happen!" cried Heidi, who knew full well what the word homesickness meant.

"We will certainly not let it die," Eric promised, his merry eyes serious again.

The excitement over the lamb had made him forget his grief, and his laughter had sounded as merrily as little Bruno's. This pleased Sally, who was now ready with her question: "May I take the lamb with me when I go visiting?"

"That depends entirely upon whom you visit," said her father with a laugh. "Heidi would welcome it, I know, and so would Peter. You may take it out to play with you and to walk with you whenever you have a free hour."

"May I, too, Papa? May I, too?" cried Bruno, beside himself with excitement.

"Yes, you may take it to the pasture to crop the grass for itself. All of you may go with it wherever you like. But never must you leave the little creature alone, not for a moment," continued the pastor. "It would run away at once, and never find its stall and miserably perish. Whoever takes it out of the stable must keep it under his eyes until he brings it back again to its place. Have you understood me well, and will you care for the lamb exactly as I have said? If you would rather not, tell me and I will ask Peter to take it back to its mother."

"No, no!" cried Eric in sudden distress. "Please don't ask Peter to take it back. I have seen how he takes care of the goats and know very well what to do. I will take care of it and never, for a moment, leave it alone. You have my word of honor."

Then all three of the pastor's children cried out that their father should leave the lamb with them. They promised from their hearts, and with all sincerity, to watch over it and care for it.

"I will, myself, see to it that the lamb is never left standing or running alone," Max promised.

But his father said that would be unsafe. It must be understood that whoever took the lamb out must bring it back again and that must be the rule.

"We will obey it."

The children gave him their hands on it, and they were all so full of excitement at the prospect of having a live lamb to keep for their very own, that they almost forgot to say good night to Peter and Heidi when it was time for them to go home.

The principal question on the following day was what name to give the lamb. After school a whole group of children met for a conference on it. Sally proposed to give it the name of Eulalia, for the cat that used to live in the parsonage was so called and the name seemed especially grand. Moreover, it brought back tender memories. But the boys wouldn't have it named for a dead cat.

"What about a dog?" asked Bruno.

He suggested the name Brave, but Max wouldn't have

*The children were full of excitement at having
a live lamb of their own*

the lamb called the same name as the dog with the broad nose who lived in the monastery and went out to rescue people in the snow.

"It would be better to name it after some hero from history. How about Hannibal?"

"But Max, Hannibal was a warrior and you promised Papa you'd forget about fighting if you had a lamb," Sally reminded him.

While they were arguing the matter, Eric was allowed to take the lamb for its first walk. The little creature was delighted and frisked and gamboled happily at his side. Heidi ran up to it and patted its curly wool and said at once, "What have they named you, little Curly Head?"

"We haven't named it yet," Eric told her. "Usually a person is called for someone, so why not a lamb?"

"Were you called for someone?" Heidi asked curiously.

Eric stopped, but not for long as the lamb was impatient to reach the slope where the grass was still green and pulled him ahead. When they were seated together on a little knoll with the lamb peacefully grazing beside them, Heidi asked again: "Were you named after someone, Eric? Bruno heard you telling the pastor that your full name is Henrico Wallerstätten. Sally told me."

"She shouldn't have listened!" Eric's blue eyes flashed angrily as he spoke.

"She didn't," Heidi defended her friend. "Bruno did, and he's too little to know better."

"He isn't too little to spread it around the school. Then the children will laugh at me and call me Velvet Knickers. My mother made that suit from her own velvet dress and I'm still proud to wear it."

And Eric went on telling Heidi about his mother and how they had lived in one place after another and how it became more and more difficult to find a house where the landlady had room for the big organ.

"My mother loved to play it and I think she would be

happy to know it is being played in church even if it is
not a church of our faith. God is the same everywhere,
she always told me. He is the shepherd and we are the
sheep of his pasture. But we were lost sheep," Eric explained. "We had to stay alone and hidden until I became
a man of honor."

"But why? I don't understand that at all," said Heidi
somewhat impatiently. "A good shepherd goes out and
finds his sheep."

"Not if he doesn't know where to look."

"You could tell him where, couldn't you? I mean the
dear Lord works through people, but if people don't
know where to look, how can they ever find you?"

"I will tell you, Heidi," answered Eric quite seriously,
"but you must promise me that you will not tell anybody, ever, even after a good many years."

"Yes, indeed, I will surely promise that," Heidi responded quickly as they ran together after the lamb. It
was tired of grazing and wanted to play a little, but Heidi
was very curious and begged Eric to tell her the secret.

"No, Heidi, you must really think it over," said Eric
and held his hands behind his back to give her time.
"Then if you are very sure that you will not say a single
word to anybody, you must give me your hand as a
promise."

Heidi was perfectly sure. "The lamb will be our wit-
ness. Just give me your hand, Eric!" she urged. "I promise you that I will not say a word to anybody about
what you are going to tell me."

Then Eric felt safe and told Heidi the secret as they
walked back towards its stall with the lamb.

"In Nolla," he began, "is a beautiful castle on a hillside
looking down on all the little houses in the village. In the
garden are beautiful flower beds full of roses and, in the
other direction there are green slopes like these around
Dörfli, where many fine horses are pastured. There is a
lake, too, and my mother loved to sit at the edge of it,
for, you see, she lived there when she was a child, and

even later. She had her own little boat to row around the lake, and beyond, where the lawn stops, come the big stables. The horses were kept there when they were not in the pasture. There were sheep, too, and Mother had her own little white pony, on which she rode around with my grandfather, or with Henrico."

"Now wait a minute!" Heidi stopped him. "You haven't told me who Henrico was. Were you named after an uncle or some other relative?"

"No, he was no relative." Again Eric hesitated. "He was the castle steward. I never knew him, you understand. He used to collect rents from the houses below and people said he was cross, but my mother loved him dearly."

"Sometimes," Heidi said, remembering how it had been with the grandfather, "all a cross person needs is someone to love him. But go on! Tell me more about the beautiful castle."

Eric went on describing everything in detail. "It was all so lovely," he finished. "I don't see how my mother could bear to leave it, but she must have loved my father very much, for she disobeyed my grandfather and ran away with him. Then he left her just as my grandfather said he would, and my mother didn't dare go back any more, and everything was all over."

Heidi had listened with the greatest attention as they walked along with the lamb between them. Now she burst forth, exclaiming: "What a shame! That is exactly like Eve in Paradise when she ate the forbidden apple. Can't you write your grandfather a letter at once and ask him if you can come home?"

"Oh, no! Oh, no! I must not do that," objected Eric. "I must not go to my grandfather until I become a man of honor, so that I can say to him, 'I will not bring any disgrace to your name, Grandfather, and Mother, through me, makes amends for the sorrow she gave you.' I promised my mother that."

"Oh, what a shame! What a shame!" mourned Heidi.

"If I had only known this when I met those children from Nolla I could have asked them about the castle. If the castle steward is still there, wouldn't he help you? My grandfather had a brother named Henrico. Could he be your castle steward?"

"It is possible," Eric admitted. "but there is no way to find out. I am bound by my promise to my mother and you are bound by your promise to me, but now that you know everything we can talk freely."

And Eric talked on and on until they reached the parsonage where Sally and her brothers were waiting for their turn with the lamb.

"Have you thought of a name for it, Eric?" all three asked at once.

"Heidi called it little Curly Head."

"But shouldn't it be named after someone?" asked Sally.

Later she consulted her father about it and he agreed that the little creature be called Curly Head after its own peculiarity, and so it was called from that time on.

CHAPTER XVII

What Keeping Silent Does

FOR A TIME the pleasure Eric took in the pretty, white Curly Head seemed to put all unhappy thoughts from his mind. In every free moment he would take the lamb out of its stall and lead it up to the pasture or to the woods.

Sometimes Heidi would go with him and he would remind her again of her promise. It seemed to keep them apart, rather than otherwise. More often it was Sally who accompanied Eric on his walks with the lamb. There was a bench at the side of the road where she would sit with the lamb's head trustfully in her lap while Eric and her brothers would run to the nearby clover field and bring some of the fine spicy leaves. Curly Head would eat them with the greatest satisfaction, first from the hand of one and then from that of the other, bleating as if to express its thanks.

At other times one of the children would go alone to take the lamb out of the stable and bring it along if some errand had to be done for Lisebeth, who seemed as fond of the lamb as the children themselves and often saved tidbits for it. Curly Head always went gladly by the side of its leader, and appeared to understand quite well what was said to it by Max and Bruno and most especially by its great friend Eric. It would answer now and then with a joyful bleat and look up at its companion so

understandingly that there was no doubt that Curly
Head took a lively part in the conversation.

Every day it became more trustful and affectionate. It
would always press close to the one who took it out of
the stall, as if its own mother had come, and the children
loved it more and more. Always, after their walks and
happy conversation, the one who took it out brought the
lamb back to its little house in the stable, and to its nice
bed of straw. With this excellent care Curly Head grew
as round as a ball, and with its snow-white curly wool
looked as pretty and clean as if it were always wearing its
Sunday dress.

Thus the beautiful, sunny autumn came to an end, and
November arrived more quickly than the pastor's children had ever known it to come before. Now they could
begin to talk about Christmas. Since the festival was little
more than a month away, Max and Bruno took constant
delight in telling Curly Head all the wonderful things
they secretly expected from the little Christ Child. Curly
Head always listened very attentively, and the brothers
assured the lamb it would surely have its share in the
Christmas presents. Eric would share in them, too, as the
pastor would not think of finding a different home for
him until after the holidays. All three boys, for the most
part, enjoyed these wonderful prospects together and
every day became more and more confidential with one
another.

Sally had a different disposition. When a new delight
was in prospect she became so excited about it, and all
her thoughts were so full of it, that the old pleasures were
a little in the background. She had come to think of
Heidi as her particular friend and the one in whom she
could confide, and she was eager to visit her and discuss
some expectations for Christmastime that her brothers, or
even Eric, who cherished such different wishes, could not
understand.

The visit was allowed, but Sally became so excited
over her plans that she hardly had patience enough to

hold still while her mother wound a warm scarf around her neck to protect her from the cold November wind. Then she bounded away and her mother watched at the window until she was nearly to the manor house, which looked quite splendid now that the carpenters had finished repairing it.

The Alm Uncle had forsaken his hut on the Alm for the more comfortable winter quarters in Dörfli, but Sally, who had expected the doctor to open the door, was a little startled to come face to face with the bearded grandfather.

"So it's Heidi you've come to visit?" he boomed back in answer to her question. "I left her up on the Alm reading to the blind grandmother, but she will be home again soon. Would you like to come inside and wait?"

"No, oh no, thank you," said Sally who would not, out of kindness, let the fierce-looking old man know he had frightened her. "I'll walk up and meet her myself."

Sally had no sooner started than it occurred to her that the way was long and it would be less tiresome to take Curly Head for a companion, if Eric or her brothers had not already taken the lamb away. She turned quickly around, ran to the stable, found Curly Head lying quietly on the straw, took it out and ran with it up the barren path now nearly covered with bright-colored autumn leaves. Running through them was delightful to both the girl and the lamb. Their continual running brought them, in a very short time to the end of their journey.

"Sally, what are you doing way up here?" exclaimed Heidi the moment she saw her.

"I came to meet you. I have so much to tell you." And Sally began a breathless account of her plans for the holidays. The Christ Child was so tiny, she explained, that he would need a little help and she was, herself, going to knit a pair of warm mittens for Eric.

"What color does he like? Has he talked to you at all?

Wouldn't it be wonderful if we found his relatives for a Christmas surprise?"

Heidi agreed that it would be wonderful, indeed, but her promise still bound her and her reply sounded less enthusiastic than Sally expected.

"What's the matter with you?" she asked. "Don't you believe in his castle any more? Max thinks he just made it up because he doesn't want people to know he's a pauper."

"I don't think he made it up," Heidi said, but she didn't explain why.

"What does Peter think?"

"I don't know. He was showing me the chickens. The grandmother has fresh eggs nearly every day."

And Heidi went on talking happily about the grandmother and how she wanted to have a little branch of evergreen on the table beside her and tie her angel on it. Heidi's plans were all about what she could give with never a word about what the little Christ Child might bring her. This gave Sally an idea and she was so filled with it that she never stopped talking until they were back at the manor house. Heidi then went in quickly and Sally ran on down the path. It was already quite dark. When she reached the parsonage, it went through her mind like a paralyzing flash:

"Where is Curly Head?"

She knew she had taken it along, then had seen it grazing contentedly on the slope just above Peter's house, but when Heidi came out and called to her, all thoughts of the lamb had left her mind. In the most terrible fright she rushed back up the mountain, calling in every direction: "Curly Head! Curly Head! Where are you? Oh, come here! Come here!"

All was still around her. No happy bleat came in answer to her call and Curly Head was nowhere to be seen. Sally ran back to Peter's house halfway up the Alm in a little hollow. There was already a light from the kitchen window and, from the little porch where she stood, she could see very well inside. They were all sitting at the table at supper, Peter, his mother, and the grandmother, who could eat nearly as well as a person who could see, but nowhere was a sign of Curly Head. Then Sally ran around the house and peeped into the goat shed. Peter's goat was there with one of the chickens roosting on its back, but there was no lamb anywhere to be seen.

Sally hesitated a moment. Should she ask Peter to help her look for it? He would be cross with her. He wouldn't want to help any girl except Heidi, and especially if the girl took him away from his supper.

Sally's anxiety increased more and more as she started back down the mountainside, always calling, "Curly Head, come here! Oh, come here!" It was all in vain; there was no sign of the lamb to be seen or heard. It grew still darker and the wind howled louder and louder, and almost blew her off the ground. How could she go home and tell that she had lost Curly Head, because she had forgotten it? Tomorrow she would tell Heidi, and they could go together and ask Peter if he had seen it.

At home everything was ready for supper, even her father was there, but they were not eating. Sally came running into the room, so disheveled that her mother said, "You cannot come to the table so, child; go and make yourself tidy."

"Above all, you must not come home so late!" her father added. "Now hurry and come right back at once or you will have nothing to eat."

Sally obeyed quickly. She suddenly felt that she would much rather not return to supper at all, but that would not do. She came back to her place dejected and frightfully anxious about what further remarks and questions would follow. But before anyone could address a word to her, the attention of all the members of the family was taken by Lisebeth. All at once she put her head in the doorway and said:

"With your permission, Pastor, although the children

are all in the house, the little lamb is not in the stable. I went out, myself, with some greens for it, and it is not there."

"What!" exclaimed the pastor. "Here's a pretty state of things! Who took it out? Who did it?"

"I didn't!"—"I didn't!"—"Surely, I didn't!"—"I didn't, either!" screamed Max, Eric, and Bruno so noisily together that no one could hear whether Sally kept silent or cried out.

"Don't be so noisy!" the mother said to quiet the boys. "It surely cannot have been Sally. In the afternoon she ran off alone to visit Heidi and only came back a few minutes ago."

"Then it is one of you three," the pastor said quickly as he cast a penetrating look towards the boys.

Max and Bruno raised a terrible outcry in reply:

"I didn't do it!" "I didn't do it!"

"I surely didn't," Eric answered, gazing at the pastor with such big, honest blue eyes that it was impossible to doubt his word.

"Then Peter must have left the stable door open," the pastor concluded. "He stopped by right after school to see how the lamb was, and it must have run out and followed him. If he finds it he will take good care of it until morning."

"But what if he doesn't find it?" the pastor's wife asked.

Suddenly Bruno laid his head on his arm and sobbed aloud, "Now Curly Head is lost! We shall never have it again. Now it will starve to death!"

Then Max began, "Yes, now it is growing colder all the time, and it won't have anything to eat and will freeze to death. How could Peter have been so careless?"

"Must you always blame Peter for everything?" asked Eric.

"That's right," Max retorted. "You are the one who usually takes it out."

"Boys!" said the pastor, and the quarreling stopped.

Then Sally began to weep and groan harder than the boys. She didn't say a word, but anyone could hear how deep her grief was from her sobs. They continued far into the night as she lay restless on her bed and could not go to sleep. Not only was she mourning for the misfortune to the lamb, now wandering about distressed and neglected in the night, but she blamed herself for keeping silent when she should have confessed. Indeed, she had not cried out: "I didn't do it! I didn't do it!" but when her mother had said confidently: "Sally cannot have done it," she had done the same wrong to keep silent, as if she had told an untruth. Sally was heartbroken and could find no rest until she made up her mind to tell Heidi all about it in the morning. Then they would go together and confess that she had lost the lamb.

In the morning there was bright sunshine, and it was at once decided that the children would go out before breakfast and look for Curly Head, for it must be somewhere about. Sally ran immediately to the manor house and, from the stone steps, called loudly: "Heidi! Heidi! Come out and help me hunt for Curly Head."

"Is the lamb lost?" asked surprised Heidi, appearing at the door. "It wasn't with you yesterday when we walked home from Peter's house, but I'll ask him about it and we can both look for it on our way to school."

"Will you look for it right now, Heidi?"

Sally knew she should have gone with Heidi as she hurried up the mountain, but Sally was expected back at the parsonage for breakfast. Her father made her feel still worse by praising her when he heard Peter was looking for Curly Head. With his experience tending goats for the whole village, there was every hope that the lamb would be found, the pastor said.

That day the whole of Dörfli and all the slopes around the village were searched, and in every home inquiries were made concerning the lamb, but it was as if Curly Head had disappeared from the earth. Nobody had seen it, nowhere was any trace of it to be found. For some days further they searched and inquired for it, but always in vain. Then the pastor said they had done enough, and it was useless to hunt any more, for either the poor little creature was no longer alive or else it had strayed far away.

Soon after this, the first snow fell, and the flakes came down so big and thick that in a short time the whole village lay deep in it, and the white covering extended to the mountain peaks and all the slopes around. Every year the children were delighted at the first snow, and always shouted and screamed the louder, the more the white flakes whirled around.

Now Sally was quite still, thinking it was too late to say anything, but always before her eyes was the sad picture of Curly Head lying somewhere under the cold snow and calling piteously for help with no one to hear its feeble bleat.

Her father came home that evening and said, "It is a bitter cold night, the snow is already frozen hard. If the poor lamb is still outdoors and not dead already, it will perish tonight. I wish I had never brought it home."

At this Eric broke into such a cry of lamentation, and Sally and her brothers joined in as if their hearts would break, that the pastor left the room and his wife tried to comfort the children by talking to them about the beautiful Christmas festival. This she did repeatedly whenever they began to mourn for Curly Head. She told them the Christ Child was coming to make every heart glad, and they must be happy, too.

"If only Curly Head wouldn't freeze to death outside, then I could be happy," Sally answered with wet eyes.

"Where is your faith?" asked her father one night when he found her kneeling beside her bed and crying as she prayed. "The dear Lord cares for all little creatures. He can prepare a warm bed somewhere for Curly Head and let all be well with it. And, although it is no longer with us, and we can't take care of it, let us be happy and give Curly Head into the dear Lord's hands."

Eric and the two brothers listened attentively while the pastor was consoling Sally, and so it came about that the boys gradually became happy again with their Christmas plans. But Sally could not be happy with them. She kept thinking, if they knew what she had done, how they would reproach her! She no longer dared look her father and mother straight in the eyes for she had let them believe for so long that she knew nothing that now she couldn't let the confession pass her lips. But on her lay, as if it were a heavy weight, the knowledge that she had kept silent when she should have spoken.

CHAPTER XVIII

What the Dear Lord Sends

NOVEMBER CAME to an end. The snow had become still deeper, and every day the cold grew more intense. The blind grandmother pulled her thin bedcovering this way and that, for she could hardly keep warm under it. The room was also cold, for Peter had wasted so much time looking for the lost lamb that there was only a small supply of wood, and in this deep snow no brushwood could be found. Coffee was seldom made as the small supply Sally had brought was used up and the beans again had to be crushed with stones; the mill was utterly useless and there was no money for a new one.

"I won't be trusted with the village goats next summer," grumbled Peter, "unless I can prove to everybody that I was not the one to lose little Curly Head."

"Who could have done such a thing? Was it Bruno, the smallest one, who took the lamb out of the stable?" Brigitte asked.

"Who knows?" Peter slammed the door as he went out, causing the whole house to tremble.

"Dear me," complained the grandmother. "I wish it had been my hearing instead of my sight that I lost."

The poor woman had much to mourn over and complain about, but most of all she missed Heidi's visits. As long as it continued to snow and the deep snow was soft, no child could get through it. There was no road broken up the mountain, and even on the other side of the slope, where Heidi and Peter had seen the merry lambkins running after their mothers, all was one vast expanse of unbroken snow.

Here there was hardship, too, for Lissa, Kurt, and little Karl were not able to sell their grandfather's baskets. Willow Joseph himself had been obliged to carry them to the dairyman, for if he had sent the children, they would have stuck fast in the drifts. Even the grandfather had trouble getting through, he sank so many times in the snowbanks.

But now the sky was clear, and the high snow fields were frozen hard far and wide, so that anyone could go over them as over a firm road. Not once, under the heaviest man, did the ice crust crack. Now the children could be sent again on their errands. Lissa wrapped a shawl around her head, Kurt and Karl put on their woolen caps, and then they started off, each with a bundle of baskets for the dairyman. After a good half hour, when they came to the chapel, Lissa put her baskets down and took each of her brothers by the hand. But Kurt was obstinate.

"I will not go in; I will not pray now. My fingers are freezing," he asserted, and planted his feet in the snow, so that Lissa could not move him forward. Karl, who always imitated his older brother, did the same.

"We keep praying for Papa to come home, and he never does, so what is the good of it?" he asked.

"But Karl, don't you want to see the crib with the Christ Child in it?" asked Lissa. "Father Klemens always puts it there early in December to remind us it will soon be Christmastime and that the dear Lord will surely send something to everyone who prays."

"He never sent us anything," both boys insisted.

They did have very little at their grandfather's house,

Lissa knew, but it still seemed to her a great consolation to kneel down and pray to a Father in Heaven who would help all poor people.

"Can't you pray a little for Mother, who is so unhappy away from our own beautiful home?" she coaxed her brothers.

Kurt at last yielded to her pleading and little Karl, still somewhat unwillingly, followed the two older children into the silent chapel. The image of the little Christ Child was there, as Lissa had promised, but it seemed odd to the observant Kurt that there was no hay in the manger as there had been the year before when they visited their grandparents and Willow Joseph brought them to the little chapel for the first time. Karl noticed it, too.

"Where is the hay?" he asked in a loud whisper.

"Be quiet," Lissa commanded him, "and say your prayers."

All three children then said their prayers softly and reverently. Suddenly a strange plaintive cry sounded through the great stillness. A little frightened, Lissa turned to Kurt and whispered softly:

"Don't do so in the chapel. You must be quiet."

Just as softly, Kurt replied, "I am not doing it. Karl is."

"I am not," Karl whispered crossly.

In a moment the cry sounded again, but louder. Kurt looked searchingly at a place by the altar. Suddenly he seized Lissa by the arm and pulled her with such force from her seat that she could do nothing but follow. Little Karl stood staring in amazement.

There, at the foot of the altar, half covered with the altar cloth under which it had crawled, lay a white lamb, trembling and shivering with cold, its thin little legs stretched out, as if it couldn't move another step, from exhaustion.

"What is that?" asked Karl who, at first, had seen only the moving altar cloth and believed it to be some kind of apparition.

"That is a sheep. Now something has been sent to us that we can see," explained Kurt with delight.

Karl's eyes grew round as saucers and Lissa, too, looked at the animal with great astonishment. The words of Father Klemens at once came to her mind, and she did not doubt that the dear Lord, who sends something to everyone who prays, had sent the lamb to them. Only Lissa didn't quite understand why it was lying there so feeble and half dead. She began to stroke the little creature, and to show it that it mustn't be afraid, but it could hardly move and only from time to time gave a very pitiful cry.

"Let's take it home and give it a potato; it is hungry," said Kurt, and little Karl began to cry, for he had often been hungry himself and hunger was the greatest evil he knew.

"What are you thinking about? We must go on up to the dairyman's," the dutiful Lissa reminded her brothers. "We have to deliver our baskets, but we can't leave the little sheep here so alone."

Kurt looked thoughtfully at the little animal breathing with such difficulty. "I know something we can do," he announced after a few minutes consideration. "Karl, you watch the lamb here, and Lissa and I will run as fast as we can up to the dairyman's and come right back and then we will take it home."

Lissa agreed to this proposal and she and Kurt immediately ran off, carrying all the baskets. Karl sat down on the floor and looked with satisfaction at his present from the dear Lord. The lamb was covered with such lovely thick wool, that shivering Karl felt a desire to put one of his cold hands into it, and it grew so warm, he quickly put in the other. Then he lay down close to the lamb and it was like a little stove for him, and although it was shivering with the cold, its woolen pelt was a splendid way for the little fellow to warm himself.

In a short time Lissa and Kurt came running back without the milk they usually carried home. They wanted their hands free in order to take their present home to show their mother that the dear Lord had sent them something even if it appeared He did not hear them praying that they might return to their beautiful home in Nolla where their father could be with them again.

"This may be a sign," Lissa announced breathlessly.

"A sign of what?" asked Karl a little fearfully.

"That we will go home and take this lamb to be with all the other sheep in the pastures of Nolla."

"It will die before that happens," Kurt predicted.

Lissa feared he was right. They tried in vain to bring the lamb to its feet. It was so weak it fell right over again.

"We must carry it," she decided at last, "but it is too heavy for me; you boys must help me." And Lissa showed them how to take hold of the lamb without hurting it, and so all three of them carried it away together. They went rather slowly, for it was quite awkward to walk with their burden, but the children were so delighted with their present from the dear Lord that they didn't stop until they reached the house under the willows where their grandparents lived. Then all three rushed in with their surprise.

"We have brought a lamb, a live lamb, with very warm wool!" little Karl cried excitedly as they entered.

When they were inside, the children placed the lamb beside their astonished mother on the bench by the stove. Then Lissa began to relate to her grandparents how it had all happened, and now it had turned out exactly as Father Klemens said, that the dear Lord sent something to everyone who prayed.

"Only today it is something we can see," broke in Kurt, jumping around it in delight.

"Be quiet!" ordered his mother. "Have you stolen the lamb? Where is the milk you were supposed to bring from the dairyman?"

"We couldn't carry it and the lamb, too, but here is the money for the baskets," Lissa explained as she placed a few coins in her grandfather's hand.

"This will buy something," he admitted, but his tone of voice told the children it would not buy very much.

"Do we have to pay the Christ Child to bring Christmas presents?" asked little Karl.

"You didn't pay for the lamb," remarked his mother, not answering his question.

"No," replied Lissa, "we found it in the chapel. Surely the dear Lord sent it to us."

"Perhaps it was the other way around," remarked Willow Joseph, "and the dear Lord sent you to the lamb."

He looked at his wife to see what she thought about it, and she looked at their daughter and said, "It is a blessing they found it."

But she couldn't see it that way. "A blessing, did you say? They pray for their father's return and the Lord sends a lamb—"

"And a sick one at that," complained their grandmother. "How are we going to feed it when there is scarcely enough for you and the children? Tell me, Joseph, where did the lamb really come from?"

After some reflection, her husband replied, "That is hard to say. Someone must go up to Father Klemens, and ask him what he thinks. I believe I will go myself." Whereupon he got up from his seat, put on his old fur cap, and went out.

Some time later Father Klemens came back with the children's grandfather. After he had greeted their grandmother and spoken a few consoling words with their mother, he sat down beside the little lamb lying there almost dead, and looked at it.

"We tried to give it some hay, but it wouldn't eat," Lissa explained, in tears now because the lamb had not responded to their care.

"Why did the Lord send us a sick lamb?" asked little Karl.

At this Father Klemens placed the three children in front of him and said, "See, children, it is so. Whenever anyone prays the dear Lord sends him a happy and a trustful heart, and that is a beautiful gift, and on it depend many other good gifts. But the lamb here has lost its way. It may belong to the big flock which passed by the chapel in September. It hardly seems it could have survived that long."

"It ate the little Christ Child's hay," explained Kurt. "Was that a sin, Father?"

"Indeed not," he replied. "The poor, innocent creature was hungry and the hay from the manger saved its life, but it may yet perish. It is too weak now to eat any more hay. First we must give it a little warm milk, and then see what more it can take."

"We will do what we can. Lissa, go and see if there is any milk left," her mother directed.

"It is all right," said kind Father Klemens. "I don't want you to deprive yourselves. If it is all the same to you, I will take the lamb home with me. There is room enough at the monastery and it will get good care."

This was a great relief to the children's grandparents, for they didn't want to let the lamb die of hunger and they didn't know where to get anything to feed it. But all three cried out that it was their present and they didn't want it taken away.

"I didn't want your father taken away either, but surely the Lord has taken him or he would have come for us," replied their mother.

At this the children cried harder than ever. They no longer wanted the lamb if it had been given to them in place of their father.

"What have we done?" cried their mother, "that such a misfortune should come to us?"

The priest comforted the poor woman and exhorted her not to give up hope. Then he took the feeble lamb on his arm and went with it up to the old monastery. But before he left he promised the children that he would do what he could to locate their father. This gave them some comfort. In all the countryside, from Maienfeld to the Swiss border, Father Klemens was the comforter of the poor, the sick and the deserted.

CHAPTER XIX

A Secret Communication

LISSA HAD quite forgotten that she had asked Heidi to pray for the return of her father. But, to Heidi, a promise was something sacred that under no circumstances ought to be broken. Not only had she promised to remember the three grandchildren of Willow Joseph in her prayers, she had also said repeatedly to Sally that she would pray for the return of the lost Curly Head.

So it happened one evening in Dörfli when the Alm Uncle and the doctor were sitting together on the seat that went all the way around the large tile stove in one room of the manor house, they heard a noise from Heidi's room just beyond.

"Listen!" said the doctor, raising his finger. "Can the child be so unhappy over the lost lamb that she sobs when she prays?"

The grandfather listened also. Had the child possibly some secret trouble? He softly opened the door a little, and heard how Heidi repeatedly prayed very urgently:

"Oh, dear Lord, don't let Curly Head die out in the cold and make it so Willow Joseph's grandchildren can go home to Nolla and please, dear Lord, find a way for Eric to go there, too, and live with his grandfather in the beautiful castle!"

Then the grandfather went in to Heidi.

"How is it," he asked, "that you have been praying to the dear Lord for these things you never mentioned to the good doctor and me?"

"I can't mention them. Never, never!" And Heidi made such an ado about it that her grandfather had to call the doctor in to quiet her.

"You really did not hear it, you did not understand it, did you, Grandfather?" exclaimed the child again and again. "You mustn't know about it, nobody must know it, it is a great secret."

"But my dear child, calm yourself and listen to me quietly," said the doctor kindly. "We heard that you were praying about something for Eric. Perhaps we can do something for him. Just tell us what you know, for it can surely be for his good."

"No! No!" cried Heidi in the greatest excitement. "I promised him that I would never tell and besides I don't know anything more than what I prayed for," and in her excitement Heidi threw herself on her pillow and began to sob.

"Lisebeth is right. We ought to have a woman in the house," said the grandfather, shaking his head as he and the doctor went out. "Was it wrong, my good friend, to interrupt Heidi at her prayers?"

"The pastor's wife can answer that better than I can," replied the doctor. "She should understand little girls. She has one of her own. Shall we go together and ask her what she thinks?"

The grandfather glanced back at Heidi's sleeping room. All was quiet now, but he did not want to leave the child alone, so the doctor went by himself and brought back both the pastor and his wife. After talking it all out, they put two things together: Eric had told the pastor that his full name was Henrico Wallerstätten and the Alm Uncle had a brother named Henrico. The name was not uncommon, but it was worth looking into. And now they had learned from Heidi's prayer that Eric might have relatives in Nolla.

"The boy must be named for someone," the doctor said.

"It would be a great blessing if we could find his relatives and my brother at the same time," agreed the Alm Uncle. "Tell me, Pastor, how shall we go about it?"

The pastor was not sure and his wife had to admit that she did not understand the little girls as well as the good doctor thought. Sally's altered behavior had not escaped her, and now Heidi, too, was sobbing as she prayed.

"They are both unhappy about something," she concluded. "Do you think they took the lamb together, secretly, and lost it?"

The Alm Uncle shook his head.

"Heidi would be praying for forgiveness if she had done that. She did pray for the lamb to be found, but she also remembered all her friends, including the grandchildren of Willow Joseph. It seems she and Peter met them the last day they went up to the high pastures. If they live in Nolla—"

"They live with Willow Joseph now. Their father has deserted them," declared the pastor. "If, by praying, Heidi could right all the troubles of the world, she would surely do so. She keeps forgetting that God works through people and if they persist in wrongdoing, her prayers can't help them. Eric could tell us about his relatives himself if he had nothing to hide."

"Couldn't we write to them?" his wife suggested. "They should be notified of his mother's death. If the grandfather is still living he will surely want to bring up his own grandson."

The pastor leaned far back in his chair and looked at his wife with amusement.

"My dear wife," he finally said, "do you really suppose I could send a letter off with the address 'To the Relatives of Henrico Wallerstätten'? For all we know they are scattered from one end of the continent to the other. Such an address might be enough for the dear Lord, but not for short-sighted human beings."

But the pastor's wife did not give up. She reminded her husband that he used to know the rector in Nolla and that his widow still lived there and wrote to them frequently. Surely she could help trace Eric's relatives. His grandfather must be lord of a manor, if not a castle, and such a person could be discovered.

When they were back at the parsonage, the pastor's sister took his wife's part and both talked so long and urgently about it that the pastor finally sat down and wrote two letters. One he addressed to the relatives of Henrico Wallerstätten. This he enclosed in the second, addressed to his friend, Mrs. Maxia Bergmann at the parsonage in Nolla. Then he placed the thick envelope on his desk, so that Lisebeth would find it early in the morning and carry it to the post office.

Lisebeth did find the letter, but she carried it only as far as the kitchen where she promptly forgot it as she fretted over other matters. Weeks had passed since Eric had come to live in the parsonage, but still she had not changed her opinion of him. She was standing full breadth in the kitchen doorway that afternoon when Eric came running up the steps and asked hurriedly:

"Where's Heidi? Has she finished her music lesson?"

Lisebeth measured him with a long look and said, "I should think a boy who came to us dressed in velvet clothes would pronounce his friend's name properly and ask: 'Where is Adelheid?' "

Eric looked at Lisebeth, frightened.

"I never knew her full name. I am sorry that I have offended you and now I will always pronounce it properly," he promised.

This did not seem at all right to Lisebeth. She had firmly believed it was Eric who had lost the lamb and that he would answer her back with the same carelessness, for which she had a suitable retort ready. Now he had answered her so politely that she was much affected, and if he should carry out his promise, the pastor's wife

might discover how she had corrected him, and that
might cause her some unpleasantness, for she knew perfectly well how tenderly the pastor's wife treated Eric.
So Lisebeth turned round and said:

"Well, you see, I always speak her name properly as I
knew her mother, Adelheid, but with you it is quite
different. You are both orphans, and for aught I care you
may call each other what you please."

"Did Heidi's mother die when she was very small?"
asked Eric, immediately sympathetic.

"Yes, I doubt that she remembers her. She was brought
up on the Alm to her grandfather when she was only
four years old."

"Thank you for telling me. I should like to ask you
something more," said Eric and waited politely for permission.

This polite manner pleased Lisebeth and she said encouragingly, "Yes, indeed, ask whatever you like."

"I want to ask if I should call you as the others do, just
'Lisebeth,' or if I should say 'Fräu Lisebeth.' "

Now Eric had won Lisebeth's whole heart, for his
considering what title she had a right to showed her what
kind of a little boy he was. She patted him on the
shoulder and said:

"Always call me just Lisebeth, and when you have
anything to ask, always come to me out in the kitchen,
and I will tell you everything that you want to
know—wait a moment!"

Whereupon she turned round and hunted a little in the
kitchen, and then came out with the letter she had forgotten.

"While you are waiting for Adelheid, why don't you
borrow her sled and carry this to the post office for me?
It's downhill all the way."

"A letter! Thank you very much, Lisebeth. I shall be
glad to mail it!" Eric exclaimed with delight as he placed
the thick envelope inside his cap and jumped on the
borrowed sled.

Lisebeth watched him with satisfaction, as if she were his grandmother, and afterwards said to the pastor, "There is a boy to be trusted. He mailed the letter and returned the sled to its owner faster than I thought possible. Now let anyone come and show me three lovelier boys in the whole world than our three."

So Eric had won everyone in his favor. There was only one who still looked at him askance and with angry eyes, and panting for revenge. A few days after Organ Sunday the justice had sent for Churi, and bold Churi could hardly stand he was so frightened, for he expected to receive a well-deserved punishment. But the justice only pinched the boy's ear a little and said:

"Churi! Churi! This time you will get off better than you deserve, for now I know perfectly well who took my Alsatian grapes last year, and know, too, who would have taken them again. From now on, if a single grape is missing, I will hold you answerable. Think about this! Now go!"

Churi did not have to be told a second time. He darted away as if his life depended on it, but from that time on he harbored revenge towards Eric, and when Eric flew past him on Heidi's sled, he shook his fist at him and said:

"Wait till I once catch you!"

But not until the day before Christmas did he meet Eric alone. Once more Eric had borrowed Heidi's sled, with Lisebeth's permission, while Heidi practiced her music lesson. From the music room came the joyful notes of a Christmas carol:

> *All my heart this night rejoices*
> *As I hear, far and near,*
> *Sweetest angel voices.*
> *"Christ is born," the choirs are singing,*
> *Till the air everywhere*
> *Now with joy is ringing.*

It did seem as if joy filled the parsonage except for one

small corner where Sally sat quite still and gave no response when her brothers came to her and begged her to come outside and play with them.

"Get your sled and we'll go coasting," urged Max. "Eric is already waiting for us at the coasting ground. Lisebeth let him borrow Heidi's sled."

"You may borrow mine if you want to," responded Sally, not moving from where she sat.

So the boys ran off, each dragging a sled behind him. Sally watched from the window, wishing she could be happy with them. But, even in her dreams, she could not escape from the pressing weight on her heart. She would see Curly Head half starved and frozen, looking up at her with sad eyes as if to say:

"You did this!"

So Sally never had a happy moment, and when Heidi finished her music lesson and came to her and said:

"Cheer up, Sally; tomorrow is Christmas, and just think of all that can happen!" tears came into Sally's eyes, and half crying, she explained that she couldn't be happy, ever again, because of little lost Curly Head.

This seemed too sad to sympathetic Heidi, and she said consolingly:

"See, Sally, when you can't do anything more, just give everything into the hands of the dear Lord, and then you will be happy again, if you haven't done anything wrong—"

"But I have done something wrong," sobbed Sally. "I took Curly Head up on the Alm that day I met you, and we were so busy talking I forgot him, and then I kept silent when my mother said, 'Sally cannot have done it,' and I am to blame for its starving and freezing and I can't be happy any more, not even at Christmastime."

Then Heidi took Sally's hand and said they would go together and confess.

"But you haven't done anything wrong. You didn't know about it," Sally protested, still sobbing.

"Yes, I have. I kept silent about something too," Heidi

told her, "and so did Eric, but Grandfather heard me praying and asked the pastor about it and he sent a letter. It was supposed to be a secret, but Eric saw the address when he mailed it, and now he thinks I broke my promise."

"He mustn't think that!" exclaimed Sally, beginning to put on her warm clothing. "Shall we go and find him? We can double up on my sled and go down in a twinkling. The 'Geiss' is a wonderfully fast sled."

"Didn't you lend it to the boys?" asked Heidi. "I saw them through the window, but Eric wasn't with them."

"He went ahead on your sled. Lisebeth told him he could borrow it. We'll probably meet him coming back," Sally said as they went out into the wintry cold and began to run towards the coasting ground.

There they joined a crowd of children, each with a sled ready to begin the long, unbroken descent down the mountainside. Once they were past the steep bit by the school they could go on without interruption until their sleds stopped by themselves on an upward slope that dipped again and, unless they were watchful, would take them all the way to Maienfeld.

As they had no sleds, Sally and Heidi waited together at the top of the coasting ground. There would be time for them to go down once or twice. Then all three of them would go to the pastor's study and tell him everything. This comforted Sally. It would be easier if she did not have to go to her father alone. Her confession to Heidi had lifted a great weight from her heart. But where was Eric and why didn't Max and Bruno come back up the hill?

"Eric! Eric!" they called once or twice, but all around them the mountain echoed back mockingly: "Rick! Rick!"

It was beginning to grow dark when Max and Bruno came back up the slope, dragging their sleds behind them. All four then shouted together to Eric, but in vain.

Two more children went past them on their way home.

"Come, we must go home, too. Perhaps Eric is already there," Max said hopefully. "He may have gone another way."

But Sally objected with all her might to this proposal, and Heidi declared firmly that there was no other way except by the road and that Eric would have come to her earlier to return her sled if something hadn't happened to prevent it.

"We must go home, anyway," Max insisted. "Come, Sally, you know we must."

"I cannot, I cannot!" wailed Sally. "You go with Bruno. Heidi and I will wait here until Eric comes. Tell Papa—"

But here Sally burst into tears and Heidi had to finish: "We three want to see the pastor. We have something to confess."

"It's about time," Max said without sympathy and left the two girls crying there in the snow while he and Bruno raced each other home.

CHAPTER XX

Very Surprising Things Happen

AT THE PARSONAGE the mother and aunt had been out in front of the house for a long time waiting for the children to come in sight. Lisebeth ran back and forth, asking the neighbors' children as they returned home, where Eric was. From them all she received the same answer: "We don't know."

Finally Max and Bruno came running through the darkness. Both were panting, one interrupting the other.

"Sally is waiting—" "Eric went down on Heidi's sled—" "They are crying—" "Eric is gone—"

"Gone where?" exclaimed the aunt.

"Come, Max, tell us calmly what has happened," the mother said, taking the older boy aside.

Then Max began telling her, very calmly, how Eric had borrowed Heidi's sled and gone down on it once or twice before the revengeful Churi saw him and gave him such a push that the sled could easily have gone over the cliff on the steep road to Maienfeld.

"Now Sally and Heidi won't come home until they find him. They said they have something to confess," Bruno finished impressively.

"For Heaven's sake!" exclaimed the mother, greatly alarmed. "I hope nothing has happened to Eric! Did all three of them have something to confess—Eric as well?"

"About the lamb, I think."

Bruno was only guessing, but Max agreed with him.

"Heidi knows nothing about it. I am sure of that," declared the aunt. "I would have heard it in her music. A violin is a sensitive instrument—"

"Yes, yes," quickly agreed the mother before the aunt could go into a longer explanation.

"It was not Eric," Lisebeth affirmed with certainty.

That left only Sally.

"The poor child may be afraid to come home. Oh, we must do something!" cried the mother.

She ran into the house to get her husband's advice while Lisebeth hurried up to the manor house to notify the Alm Uncle and the doctor. They returned immediately with seven or eight neighbors in the midst of a great uproar, all armed with big poles and lanterns, as they wanted to make sure Eric had not fallen over the cliff. Then the pastor came out and joined the procession, for he had to persuade Sally and Heidi to come home. Last of all came Lisebeth, with a great basket on her arm, for she never went out anywhere without a basket.

Two long hours passed, during which the pastor's wife went restlessly first to the window, then to the front door, then up to her bedroom and down again, for the longer she was without any news the greater became her distress. Finally the front door opened and in stepped her husband with weeping Sally by one hand and Heidi by the other. They had confessed everything, but he had not been able to console them.

"If I had told about the lamb it wouldn't be lying out in the snow somewhere stiff and frozen," sobbed Sally.

"And if I had told about Eric he might be home with his grandfather in the beautiful castle," Heidi said in the midst of copious tears.

Up to that time no trace of Eric had been found. Heidi was allowed to stay with Sally while the grandfather, the doctor, and all the neighbors kept on looking for him.

Lisebeth was still with them, the most eager of all in the search for lost Eric.

"It's all our fault for keeping silent," Sally and Heidi sobbed together.

After many comforting words from Sally's mother, and after Sally and Heidi had both prayed from their hearts for the dear Lord to forgive them and not let Eric be lost like poor little Curly Head, the two children were finally calmed and went to sleep.

Christmas morning passed silently and sadly in the parsonage. The girls slept until late, for which everyone was glad, as their great trouble would have wakened with them. Eric had not yet been found and the church was filled with weary neighbors who had decided there was nothing left for them to do but pray.

At home Max and Bruno had kept very quiet, Max with a large book on his knees, Bruno busily interested in breaking off the guns from his lead soldiers, as now it was peacetime.

"Well," said Max seriously, as he looked up from his book, "if the Christ Child brings you that fort you've been wishing for, you will have no more weapons with which to defend it."

Bruno had not thought about this. He quickly threw all the weaponless men into the box and said, "I will not do anything more today," evidently with the silent hope that Eric would be found.

Max, who through the window had seen the great gathering by the church, did not care to stay indoors any longer, as he wanted to hear what was going on out there. The aunt objected for some time, but finally gave permission for half an hour, with his mother's agreement, as she had just come in. Then Sally appeared and at once threw herself stormily on her mother, asking what had happened about Eric, and Heidi joined in, wanting to know who had found him, and how, and where, and when.

Before the pastor's wife had time to tell the two who

had just awakened that there was no news of Eric, but that early that morning still more people had set out to look for him, Sally's two brothers came rushing in and called out together:

"Here comes a tall, tall—"

"A very tall gentleman—"

"A very erect gentleman in a carriage with two horses."

"He looks like my grandfather," Heidi observed, rushing to the window and pulling Sally along with her. The doctor had come for Heidi, but Sally didn't want her to leave until they found out a little more about the strange visitor who looked like the grandfather without his beard.

"I believe he is a general," Max finally burst out importantly.

"Without doubt," laughed the aunt. "Next thing you will see the real old Carthaginians wandering around in all Dörfli and the vicinity."

But the doctor did not laugh. "May it not be someone bringing news of Eric?" he asked the pastor's wife.

Then Heidi knew he had not been found and clung to Sally. Could this be their punishment for keeping silent when they ought to have spoken? They asked the doctor about it and he reminded them that a God of love does not punish.

"Have you forgotten what you yourself said to me up in the high pastures?" he asked Heidi. "You told me I must wait and keep thinking, 'Surely now the dear Lord knows some joy which is to come out of this trouble?'"

"My mother said that, too," Sally put in. "She told me every heart would be glad at Christmastime."

"And so it will," agreed the doctor. "We will see to that ourselves. The Christ Child brings love into all our hearts at Christmastime, and with love much can be accomplished."

Heidi lingered a moment more at the window to think

about this. Waiting below, she could see an open traveling carriage with runners like a sled. The two black
horses hitched to it were impatiently pawing the ground
and shaking their harness so that it made a loud clanging
like Christmas bells. This sound was irresistible to Max
and Bruno, who immediately ran outside again.

Then, just as Heidi and the doctor left, Lisebeth came
in and announced:

"There is a strange gentleman down with the pastor. I
showed him in there, so that the table could be laid here,
for I must go out after the little boy again. The gentleman
says he came in response to the pastor's letter."

"And did he come alone, without Eric?" asked the
pastor's wife. "Who can he be?"

Her question was being answered below in the study
as the strange, tall gentleman stepped inside, introducing
himself as Henrico Halm, steward of the Castle Wallerstätten and sent by the Baron from Nolla.

The pastor was so surprised that for a moment he
could hardly collect himself. There stood before him a
man whose existence had been little more than a myth,
and he looked so stately and imperious that he could
command respect from anyone. But there was something
at the same time in his expression which the pastor recognized as exactly like the Alm Uncle's when all the villagers had feared him. How could he tell such a man, who
must have been sent to fetch the Baron's grandson, that
Eric had disappeared?

These thoughts went through the pastor's mind
quickly, for the visitor did not give the surprised pastor
much time to recover himself. He seated himself in the
offered chair, drew the pastor down into another, looked
him in the eyes, and said:

"My dear Pastor, I would not have come to Dörfli for
myself. But you sent the Baron of Castle Wallerstätten,
through the mediation of the rector's widow in Nolla, a
communication of which I do not believe one word."

The pastor's surprise showed in his face.

"Not that I think you would tell an untruth," the speaker continued, "but you have, yourself, been deceived. Back of all this is a crafty man who wants to outwit the Baron for profit. I have, for many years, protected him from all such schemes. So here I am, and I will tell you anything you wish to know about the misfortune which has led to this deception. But first let me see the child this man dares to place before the Baron as his grandchild."

Then the pastor had to tell him of Eric's disappearance, how up to now they had searched for him in vain, but that everything would be done to find him.

"My good Pastor, don't let them hunt any further; the boy will not be seen again," declared the tall visitor. "The man who has played into your hand has made a mistake this time. He really hoped the Baron would come himself and that he could place some foundling before him as his daughter's child. Instead, the Baron sent me. That is why the child has disappeared, my dear Pastor. He knows he can't fool the Castle Steward."

The pastor then tried to say that there was no man, but only a motherless little boy who had come to live at the parsonage, but a knock on the door interrupted him. Heidi, encouraged by the doctor, had hurried home and returned with her grandfather. The two were admitted and, for a moment, there was utter silence in the room as they faced each other, their faces working strangely. Suddenly tears came to the Alm Uncle's eyes as he cried, "Henrico! Is it really you?"

"He is the Castle Steward, Grandfather. Didn't you hear him say so while we were waiting outside the door?" asked Heidi. "Eric told me about him, but I didn't dare tell anybody because he said he wouldn't go to his grandfather until he was a man of honor. He promised his mother that."

"Well, the boy has at least found a good friend and defender," said Henrico. "So this is your grandfather, little one? My brother is more fortunate than I am. Has anyone told you that I am your uncle and a lonely old man with no grandchildren of my own?"

"You won't be lonely any more," declared the Alm Uncle. "You are invited to spend Christmas with us. There will be a big festival at the parsonage—as soon as Eric is found. Then you will see for yourself what a fine boy he is."

"Well, I must say, he has fallen into good hands, whoever he is, and I thank you for your invitation. But I have promised the Baron to be with him, so I really must take my leave. I won't forget you, Brother," he continued as he and the Alm Uncle walked vigorously along the hall, followed by Heidi, who had tried in vain to get ahead of them to open the outside door as politely as Eric had once done for her. But, before the door could be opened from the inside, it was pushed open from the outside with great force, and like an arrow, small Bruno shot straight into the tall Castle Steward, and immediately Max ran into Bruno, and the surprised gentleman received a second push, while a bewildering screaming of confused voices fell on his ears:

"They are coming!"—"Here they come!"—"Lisebeth found Eric!"—"No, it was Father Klemens!"

Soon Lisebeth appeared at the door, very broad in her Sunday attire, with Eric by the hand. Behind these two followed a crowd of sympathetic school children, among them Churi, who seemed most attentive of all. No further advance was possible for the Castle Steward. He yielded and retreated, step by step, until he came backwards over the threshold into the study again, together with all the pastor's family and the Alm Uncle. Last of all struggling Heidi pushed in, having grasped Eric's other hand. Everyone wanted to hear the whole story of Eric's having been lost and found again, who found him and all about it.

When, through strenuous efforts, Heidi succeeded in drawing Eric and Lisebeth out of the crowd and into the study, enough quiet resulted so that they could be understood, for the school friends remained standing respectfully in front of the door, as they did not dare crowd into the pastor's study.

Then, at last, Eric told how, after a hard push, his sled went so far he couldn't tell where he was. He began dragging it up the road he thought went back to Dörfli. Actually it led to the fortified mountain pass across to Lichtenstein, but long before he reached the top he found himself too tired and chilled to go on.

"Then what happened?" asked Heidi as more children pressed forward to hear all about it. Peter was among them. He had been out with the searchers all night.

"I didn't find Eric," he told Heidi in a low voice, "but I was the first to find out about the lamb."

"Don't tell Sally. She will be heartbroken. Is it quite dead?" asked Heidi, her face turning very white.

"It is not dead at all," replied Peter, delighted that he could bring the glad news to Heidi. "Father Klemens says it is round and full and jumping around so merrily that the monks will be sorry to see it go, but you are not to tell Sally that, either. We have planned it for a Christmas surprise."

CHAPTER XXI

And Every Heart Is Glad

MORE SURPRISES were planned. Heidi could feel it in the air and see it in all the happy faces. In the general excitement and delight over Eric's safe return, she had forgotten to tell Peter about her Uncle Henrico. He had dropped down unnoticed into a chair beside the grandfather where he listened attentively as first Eric and then Lisebeth brought out the story of his rescue by a strange man who was on his way home for Christmas.

"He found me and wrapped me in blankets and took me to his house under the big willows," Eric finished. "Then, in the morning, he called Father Klemens and Lisebeth met us and so here I am. I'm sorry I couldn't return Heidi's sled right away."

"Did Churi push you very hard?" asked Peter, glaring at the silent but attentive Churi.

"He didn't mean it. We're good friends now," declared Eric. "I don't care if he does call me Velvet Knickers. My mother made those clothes out of velvet she brought from the castle and I shall always be proud to wear them."

"That's the spirit," said a voice from the corner.

Then Eric noticed, for the first time, the strange gentleman beside the Alm Uncle. When he beckoned to him, Eric obeyed at once.

"Come here, my boy. There, look me straight in the eyes and tell me your name," he directed as Eric stood politely in front of him.

"It is Henrico Wallerstätten, sir, but I am called Eric Wall," he replied without hesitation.

The gentleman looked at him still more closely.

"After whom were you called, my boy, do you know that?"

Eric did not turn his clear blue eyes away from the gentleman as he replied, "After the Castle Steward, sir, the one who used to lead my mother's white pony."

"My boy—your mother looked at me so when she was your age. I am the Castle Steward and I have found my brother here, and his little granddaughter—" and then great tears ran down the austere gentleman's cheeks.

When Eric noticed this a sad thought rose to his mind, and he said, quite cast down:

"I would like to live with my grandfather, too, but I cannot go to him, not for a long, long time. When I am a man of honor I may go to the castle and say to him: 'My mother sends me so that I may do honor to the name Wallerstätten and atone for the sorrow she brought you when she disobeyed you and ran away to marry a man against your wishes.'"

Henrico then put his arm affectionately around Eric and said, "There is no difference now, no difference at all. You are not the only one who took the wrong road, my boy, but now everything is all right. Your grandfather meant well, but a young girl must sometimes obey her heart instead of her father."

Eric thought about this for a minute. It seemed to distress him. Then he said, "But I must obey my mother. I cannot go to my grandfather now."

"You will not be disobeying her in the least for, you see, you will not go to your grandfather. He will come to you. I shall see to that," declared the Castle Steward, "and you shall become a man of honor, too."

"Yes, and I know how to do it, too. It was in my

mother's song. She used to play the big organ that is in the church now and we would all sing for the blind grandmother. It made her happy to the very last. Could we sing it now?" Eric asked, turning around to see if Heidi and Peter were there. Then the pastor's wife came into the room.

"Children," she said, beckoning with her finger, "in there the lights are burning by the piano. Now we are all going to sing some Christmas carols. Where is Sally?"

In the twilight her mother had not noticed that Sally was sitting in a corner not making a sound. Now she came out, and all went over to the piano. A violin, in a shiny new case, was waiting for Heidi to play.

"Please," Sally begged, "don't play 'Little Lambkins.' I couldn't bear it now."

Heidi was tempted to tell her, but she couldn't spoil the surprise. Then the aunt sat down and played, expecting Heidi to accompany her on the violin. But Heidi had seen the tag, HEIDI FROM KLARA, and was too overjoyed to do anything but hug the instrument while happy tears dropped from her eyes.

"Now!" said Fräulein, trying to be the severe music teacher and failing utterly. "Shall we begin?"

Then, taking up her new violin and drawing the bow very gently over the strings, Heidi played the one carol she had learned:

> *All my heart this night rejoices*
> *As I hear, far and near,*
> *Sweetest angel voices.*
> *"Christ is born," the choirs are singing,*
> *Till the air everywhere*
> *Now with joy is ringing.*

Eric and Peter joined in, just as they had done when Eric's mother was playing the organ, and sang at the top of their voices, but Sally couldn't rejoice when she still believed little Curly Head had perished somewhere outside in the snow. She couldn't share Heidi's pleasure in her new violin or her excitement when she spoke of playing it for the blind grandmother.

"She'll like the part about the angel voices because of the angel I brought her from the Gemmi. It was my guardian angel," Heidi said, "but it was really Seppli who saved me by leading the men to the bush with the red flowers."

Peter had forgotten about Seppli and that, in a jealous mood, he had said he hated him. There was no hatred in anyone's voice now, only love and the happy excitement of freshly awakened hopes. Then the doorbell rang louder and louder, and Bruno, jumping up and down with delight, exclaimed, "The Christ Child!"

Immediately the door was opened and a flood of light came in from outside. As all the children rushed towards it, the splendor streamed and shimmered and sparkled all around as a big fir tree was carried in and placed there, in the middle of the big room. Bright lights glistened from top to bottom on all the branches, and rosy angels and shining summer birds hovered around the lights, and red strawberries, and shining cherries, and golden pears and little apples hung from all the twigs. Then the children formed a circle and danced and pulled each other this way and that to see each new wonder. But all at once something came running in and suddenly Sally almost collapsed and—really, there was little Curly Head! Round as a ball, lively and roguish, it rushed at each one of the children in turn, rubbed its head against each one and bleated loudly for joy. Sally could hardly believe what she saw. Curly Head, neither hungry nor frozen but quite alive and merry, was there again! "How can it be?" she kept asking, but everyone was too excited to answer.

Now Bruno caught sight of something and gave a high jump. "Max! Max!" he screamed. "The fort! The fort!" But Max had already jumped to the other side and called back, "Here is the new sled! Now Eric won't have to borrow Heidi's sled any more. And look at the box of colors! Oh, so many brushes in it!"

Heidi kept hugging her violin

Heidi kept hugging her violin in its shining case and thinking of Klara, who had guessed her dearest wish. Now she could carry it up on the Alm and play so many tunes for the blind grandmother. Oh, how happy she was now, not only for herself but for all her friends! Everything that had troubled them was past. The dear Lord had worked it all out, bringing joy into everyone's heart.

All at once Heidi saw two eyes, wide open, gazing at the shining tree in silent wonder. Could that be Seppli all the way from the Gemmi? But no, this boy was not so round as Seppli. Where had she seen him? Then she remembered. There were all three of Willow Joseph's grandchildren standing beside the tree and looking in astonishment at all the brilliant splendor. Heidi went to them.

"Did you really come to see me, Lissa?" she asked the oldest child. "Isn't the tree beautiful? Did you know the Christ Child would come today?"

"Oh, no! Oh, no!" said Lissa quite shyly and softly, "but our father came home with Eric and when Father Klemens came, he discovered that the lamb belonged to you, and said we might bring it here."

"But where was it?" asked Sally, hoping to receive an answer from these strange children. "Did you know about it, Heidi?"

"Only just now when Peter told me. Did you find it and take it to Father Klemens?" asked Heidi. "Where was it?"

"In the chapel," Lissa and Kurt replied both together, and little Karl added, "The Christ Child sent it. We found it by his manger, but it wasn't wrong for the lamb to eat the hay. Father Klemens said so."

Then the pastor's wife came in and said the children would tell them all about it later, but now she must bring them to the table by the window, for the Christ Child had remembered them, too. But at first no urging could move them from the spot, for they had never seen such a shining tree with lights on every bough. Finally Lissa said, "We had a little tree once at home in Nolla, but this year our father brought Eric home when he found him in the snow."

The father then stepped forward to explain: "I am but a poor carpenter with no work and no money. If I hadn't found the boy I might have been ashamed to come home empty-handed."

The blind grandmother's words came back to Heidi, and she said, "You brought yourself. That was what your children wanted most."

"You're a carpenter, did you say? Would you consider working in Nolla?" asked the Castle Steward, who was still there watching the festivities.

"Nolla is my home, but there is no work. The castle is falling to pieces—"

"The Baron will see to it that everything is in good repair before he comes for his grandson. What do you say, Eric? Finish the school term here and then come with my niece Heidi, and my brother Tobias. Will you do that?" asked Heidi's newly discovered uncle.

Eric said he would, but Heidi had to think about it. At first she didn't recognize Tobias as her grandfather's name. He had been simply Grandfather or the Alm Uncle for so long. But then she told herself that once these two had been brothers, like Max and Bruno. Probably Henrico had followed Tobias and tried to be like him. It was all very strange and exciting. Maybe, someday, she could express how she felt on her violin.

But now the children were all being led to the table. Karl moved slowly, not taking his eyes away from the tree. But the table gave him a sight he had not expected. On a plate lay the largest gingercake he had ever seen, and around it lay red apples and a big pile of nuts. Peter joined the younger boys as soon as he had put the lamb safely in its stall. His best gift was to be cleared of blame for losing it. Now he could eat with a good appetite again.

"Peter," Heidi called from under the tree while he was still enjoying his gingercake. "Here is a package for you. Aren't you going to open it?"

Inside was a good strong jacket such as Peter had never owned in his life. Then two warm blankets came in sight, but there seemed to be a hard object in the middle of them. Peter lifted it and his blue eyes shone with delight, for his wish had been fulfilled. He held up a brand new coffee mill for everyone to see. Now at last he could grind the coffee properly and not have to depend on stones.

"How pleased the grandmother will be!" exclaimed Heidi. "And Peter, here is a strong knapsack in which we can carry some of the apples and nuts. Shall we go at once and show your mother and grandmother what the Christ Child has brought?"

"If you go past the chapel, don't forget to go in and pray, for you know the dear Lord always sends you something," said little Karl, who had noticed that all the rich gifts of this day were connected with the lamb they had found in the chapel.

"These gifts are from our friends," Heidi explained, "but it was the dear Lord who put the love in their hearts and when they thought of the little Christ Child they knew it was time for giving."

"I couldn't have explained it better myself," declared the pastor. "The chapel is for anyone in need. The lamb understood that. No difference in faith divides God's smaller creatures. Let no differences divide us from now on."

"Amen," said Peter who, for once, thoroughly agreed with the pastor.

But now it was time for Henrico to leave. There was much he had to tell the Baron. Turning to the three grandchildren of Willow Joseph, he asked: "How would you like to go home to Nolla in my carriage? We will say good-bye to your grandparents when we stop for your mother. I'm sure it won't take her long to pack.

There is work to be done at the castle as soon as I say the word."

"Are we going now?" Karl's eyes grew bigger and bigger with wonder and expectation. Lissa and Kurt ran off shouting for joy, to seat themselves in the luxurious carriage. Eric stood for a moment, wishing he could go with them. Then he said bravely, "I can wait."

"Of course you can, boy. Your grandfather will come for you. Never doubt it. But if he remains stubborn, I will come for you myself," Henrico promised, "and Heidi, too. I'm expecting a visit from my brother."

"Can we take Sally, too? And Max? And Bruno?"

The Castle Steward laughed at that. "I could wish for nothing better, my boy, but we can't suddenly rob the parsonage of all its children. Who would take care of the lamb?"

"I'll never forget it again," declared Sally. "It really is my present from the Christ Child because Lissa and Kurt and Karl found it by his manger. Good-bye and come again!"

"We will! We will!" cried the children as their father joined them in the carriage.

And thus they traveled to the distant castle.